The Night Train

The Night Train

A Novel

Clyde Edgerton

Little, Brown and Company
NEW YORK   BOSTON   LONDON

Little, Brown and Company
Hachette Book Group
237 Park Avenue, New York, NY 10017
www.hachettebookgroup.com

First Edition: July 2011

Little, Brown and Company is a division of Hachette Book Group, Inc. The Little, Brown name and logo are trademarks of Hachette Book Group, Inc.

The characters and events in this book are fictitious. Any similarity to real persons, living or dead, is coincidental and not intended by the author.

The publisher is not responsible for websites (or their content) that are not owned by the publisher.

Library of Congress Cataloging-in-Publication Data
Edgerton, Clyde.
    The night train : a novel / Clyde Edgerton. — 1st ed.
        p. cm.
    ISBN 978-0-316-11759-3
    1. Musicians — Fiction.   2. African American musicians — Fiction.
3. Male friendship — Fiction.   4. Interracial friendship — Fiction.
I. Title.
    PS3555.D47N54 2011
    813'.54 — dc22   2010041546

10 9 8 7 6 5 4 3 2 1

RRD-IN

Printed in the United States of America

For Nathaniel Hart Edgerton

PART I

1

Friday, April 12, 1963

THE BOY LEANED in at the open front door of the bar. From inside, he looked like a dark stamp on the bright daylight behind him. A hemophiliac called the Bleeder sat in an armless chair on a small, low bandstand, an electric guitar strapped around his neck. He was alone and had been practicing his music. Come on in here, he said to the boy.

The back door of the bar was also open. Scents of pine and wisteria mixed with the smell of stale beer.

The name of the bar was the Frog. It sat near the train switching station just north of Starke, North Carolina—and was the only regular jazz spot within a hundred miles. The Bleeder played standard jazz tunes with four white men on Friday nights. The Jazz Group.

The boy advanced slowly past the pinball machine and a stack of chairs.

The Bleeder thought of that song "Roun'headed Boy": *Roun'headed boy, sneaking through the shed, / Thinking he clear of the shucks and the dread / That's soon to fall like the thick night rain, / Drowning out the whistle of the northbound train.*

He noticed the boy looking at the piano, a Fender Rhodes electric. Sit down on that piano stool, he said. You like music?

Yessuh.

What's your name?

Larry Nolan.

How old are you?

Sixteen.

Nolan? thought the Bleeder. He remembered something about that family with the *names*. What's your *whole* name? he asked.

Larry Lime Beacon of Time Reckoning Breathe on Me Nolan. He raised an eyebrow. They call me Larry Lime.

Good Lord. Who name you all that?

Aunt Marzie, my grandma. She name us all.

Can you play that Rhodes?

Rhodes?

That piano.

Larry Lime looked at the keys. A little bit, he said. A lady at church showing me some stuff.

Which church?

Liberty Day A.M.E.

You know scales?

Yessuh. Some.

Well, play me a B-flat scale on there, up two octaves and back. Left hand.

I ain't tried a B-flat that much. I can do a C, G, or F.

Do one.

Larry Lime played the C-major scale up and back.

Okay. Now play me a tune.

Larry Lime played "What a Friend We Have in Jesus," one-finger bass notes with the left hand, a straightforward arrangement. It was steady, no mistakes.

That's good. I can get you doing that one like Professor Longhair. Then like some other people.

The Bleeder started in on something, tapping his heel and playing guitar, and on top of it he started singing "What a friend we have in Jesus." Larry Lime had never heard the likes. It didn't just move up and down; it moved out and back.

Can you do a C-minor scale? asked the Bleeder.

I can't do no minors yet.

Let me just show you something. He lifted his

guitar and strap from around his neck, placed the guitar on its stand, slid his chair over, and played an E blues scale on the piano. Can you play that? he said. It ain't but se'm notes. E blues.

The Bleeder wore dark, loose clothes. Don't worry about no fingering, he said. Just hit the notes. He smiled enough for Larry Lime to see his gold tooth.

Larry Lime played, got it right. He liked the slanted sound.

Look, now. Watch this. Just play around with those notes like this.

Larry Lime played it. It was more like a tune than a scale.

Okay, now you keep on doing that, right there in E, but play it in a little pattern sort of like this, like this here...and I'll do a little...a little move with the guitar. He picked up the guitar, turned down the amp a notch, played along with Larry Lime.

Larry Lime's eyes stayed on his hands, but his face reflected a crystal ball. They played the last few notes together.

I'm the Bleeder. That's what they call me. You got a lot to learn. I'll teach you some stuff.

The Bleeder had seen the boy and the man outside before—come to get the trash. Y'all got that pickup truck with plywood sides?

Yessuh.

Is he your daddy?

My cousin, but everybody call him Uncle Young.

Aunt Marzie name *him* too?

Yessuh.

What's *his* whole name?

Young Prophet of Light and Material Witness to the Creation Trumpet Jones.

That's a good one. What your daddy's name?

Booker.

No long name, huh?

Nossuh, but my mama got one.

What's that?

Canary Bird in the Shopwindow of Love Jones Nolan.

How come you know all the names?

We say 'em a lot.

Where you practice your music?

In the furniture shop where I work, and at church.

What's your grandma's name — the one that name everybody?

Her name Marzie Elizabeth Cotton Barbara Jane Flower in the Meadow Jones.

My goodness. He picked up a rag from his guitar case, wiped down his strings. Listen, you gone have to learn all the scales, every one, so you can play with horns and you'll feel comfortable anywhere on the piano. You got to think about moving into some stuff on beyond what you doing in church, if you up for it. Now look, let me show you this on the scales — the regular scales. You can do any fingering you want. You can cross over the fifth finger with the fourth. See? You cross your thumb under your first finger if you want to. And I'll start you slow. You can forget all that other you been learning, but you can use it too. I got a book you can use. Now play me a C chord.

Larry Lime played a triad.

Okay. One, three, five. Can you do the next variation up?

Variation?

Nevermind. Can you come back here next Friday?

Yessuh. We come by every Friday.

I'll branch you out a little 'fore I get shed of you. Stick a six in that C chord.

A six?

Yeah. The sixth note in the C scale, a A. Okay, now what you got to learn is you can stick a two in there, or a seven, say. You got a whole bunch you can throw in there, and you can take out any of them — the one especially, 'cause a bass man taking care of that — and you got to listen for all the different colors and feels you get from the different combinations, and you got to learn chord variations in all twelve keys. And this mean you got to practice yo' ass off. You up for that?

Larry Lime looked at the Bleeder. Yessuh.

I don't mean practice yo' ass off, I mean practice yo' ass *off*, practice yo *ass* off. The Bleeder's eyebrows were raised. His head leaned forward. He looked over at the door.

A man leaned against the doorjamb.

Hey, come on in, said the Bleeder.

Uncle Young broke from leaning against the doorjamb, walked in. Hey there, he said and put out his hand to the Bleeder. Then he said to Larry Lime, What you doing in here?

He showing me some stuff on the piano.

I'm the Bleeder.

Yeah, I heard of you. I'm Young.

He's pretty good. Can he stay a little bit?

Uncle Young asked Larry Lime, You want to walk home?

Yessuh.

All right wid me. I take the haul to the dump.

2

AFTER HIS LESSON, Larry Lime walked along Prestonville Road. He hummed intervals — a second, then a third — walked across a ditch and onto the tracks, headed south, not far below the train switching yard. Stopped trains divided Starke for as long as thirty minutes sometimes, stretched warm in the sun or cool under the moon, like a resting snake.

As he walked, Larry Lime was trying to feel, see, to somehow experience a different color for each interval. Next lesson, if his mama said it was okay to go back, he was going to have to listen to an interval and then say what it was: fifth, sixth, and so forth.

He didn't try to walk a rail like he often did.

If from the sky above the tracks where Larry Lime

walked you looked down, as a crow facing north might, you'd see off to your left and Larry's right—to the west of the north–south track—a community of 67 clapboard homes and a brick church. To the east of the tracks: 124 homes, several stores, a large dog food factory, and Starke School—grades one through twelve. The consolidated school would open in two years. Through East Starke, north–south, was Prestonville Road, a two-lane blacktop. Through West Starke, also north–south, was a dirt road, Luther's Chin Road.

Two other dirt roads, the North Cut and the South Cut, crossed the tracks at ninety-degree angles (almost), as did several footpaths.

From the crow's altitude, you'd see the college town of Whittier, five miles north of Starke. Whittier College, sometimes called *communist*, stressed liberal arts. A black college was there too—Cresstead College. Seven miles to the south was Prestonville, where a chapter of the Ku Klux Klan met monthly. It was a large chapter for North Carolina, though in those days not particularly large for, say, Alabama, Georgia, South Carolina, or Mississippi.

Before reaching the South Cut, Larry Lime started to take a footpath that ran behind the church and toward his house. But he stopped, glanced east along the path that led to the back of Mr. Hallston's furniture shop—where he worked refinishing furniture on the afternoons he didn't ride with Uncle Young on the trash pickup or on the meat run.

He heard a late-day train, looked south along the track, and saw the engine headlight far away, bright in the early evening, shining its figure-eight pattern.

He looked back toward the shop, saw Dwayne, Mr. Hallston's son, behind the shop doing something. They worked together most afternoons. Dwayne was setting up a line of tin cans in front of a dirt bank. He held his .22 rifle in his hand.

Dwayne's shepherd-retriever mix, Dusty, lay behind the shop, watching.

The furniture shop had two rooms. One was the big refinishing room where Larry Lime, Dwayne, and another worker or two, including the foreman, Flash Acres, stripped paint and lacquer from chairs and tables, then sanded, smoothed, and applied refinishing liquids to them. Two tall cotton-gin fans stood in this room. Weather permitting, stripping and painting were done outside. The smaller shop room in back, the storage room, held an old upright piano—a Darnell & Thomas, the boiler plate reading: "established 1887, Raleigh, N.C., with improved patent French repeating action, quality of the highest order."

Larry Lime noticed the crows up in the trees rais-

ing a fuss about something. He walked toward Dwayne.
Hey, man, he said. He threw up his hand.

Dusty stood, stretched, walked out to meet him.

Hey. Dwayne stood holding the .22 in one hand, the
barrel pointed down. It was a bolt-action, single-shot.
I'm shooting from the hip like the Rifleman, he said.

Yeah, the Rifleman, said Larry Lime.

Dwayne turned, leveled the gun at his waist, and
fired at the tin cans. He hit short, in the dirt. Dusty
found his spot, lay back down. Larry Lime sat on an old
sawhorse that had been moved out of the shop. The train
was almost to the South Cut, not moving very fast.

Dwayne didn't quite know if he should ask Larry
Lime to shoot or not. He wondered if Flash Acres had
left for the day. Sometimes he stayed late.

Them crows, said Larry Lime. They got crows in
that movie *The Birds*. You seen that?

Yeah, me and Mickey Dean took dates last weekend. That was something, man. You seen it?

I ain't seen it yet.

It's better'n *Psycho*. Did you see *Psycho*?

Yeah, I saw that, said Larry Lime. That man and
his mama, and that stuff in the shower, man. All that
blood sucking down the drain. My girlfriend screamed
like crazy. I got a idea about dropping a rooster outen
the balcony.

What you mean? Dwayne fired again from the waist, missed low again.

I mean sneak a rooster up in the balcony under a overcoat and sit on the front row, and about the time them birds getting ready to peck somebody in the eye, you throw that rooster out in the air and let him fly down on somebody's head. We got a rooster at the house we got to get shed of.

Dwayne opened the rifle chamber. *Man, oh man,* he thought. *What a great idea!*

Larry Lime's cousin, Uncle Young, at the last family gathering, said, I want to see a rooster at that birds movie turned loose from the balcony and flap all down in them white people's hair right when something scary's going on.

The train was moving by, clanking and groaning, about fifty yards away, the cars showing "Southern Pacific," "Atlantic Coast Line," "Central of Georgia." The whistle blew for the North Cut, echoing in the woods.

I'm gone do it with our rooster, said Larry Lime, when it come to West Preston, maybe.

That would be in the colored theater, thought Dwayne. He said, Why don't you do it in Whittier — at the Rialto?

I ain't gone mess with that.

Dwayne visualized the scrambling — people trying to get away from a flapping chicken right when those little school children are running along and the crows are dropping down out of the sky. Maybe, said Dwayne, I could cover for you somehow. He immediately regretted saying it.

What you mean?

I don't know. I could say I saw somebody else do it. Or I could bring in the chicken. At the Rialto. Not down in Prestonville.

I don't know, said Larry Lime. But I know we got to get shed of our rooster. He's a mean bastard. And I know how to make him go to sleep, 'cept he might not stay asleep too long.

How's that?

Tuck his head under his wing, swing him back and forth. Larry Lime demonstrated.

Dwayne shot from the waist, hit below the cans again. You still teaching that other chicken to dance? he asked.

She done trained good. Redbird. I got her doing it on a flat, round pan now. She funny. Larry Lime looked at the tin cans and said, Uncle Young say you just act like you point your finger at something.

Dwayne, from his waist, pointed his finger at the cans. How long will they stay asleep when you do that head under the wing thing? he asked.

Five minutes or so. Something like that.

You want to shoot? said Dwayne.

Yeah, I'll shoot.

Dwayne looked past the furniture shop to his house. Nobody looking. He said, We could figure out where would be the best part in the movie to drop the chicken. How many minutes in. *Or,* thought Dwayne, *how come Larry Lime's got to be in on it?* No need to chance that. Mickey Dean would want to help Dwayne drop the chicken.

Larry Lime shot from the waist, hit the bank above the tin cans.

Dwayne asked, How about if I borrow your rooster?

Okay. But I'd have to show you how to put him to sleep. He handed the gun back to Dwayne.

Can you bring him to the shop? asked Dwayne.

Sure. When?

Sometime soon. Dwayne aimed from the shoulder, shot. A tin can jumped into the air.

You do it at the white theater, and I'll do it at the colored, said Larry Lime.

That's a deal.

Dwayne's mother called him from their back porch.

I got to go eat, said Dwayne. I see you, man.

Dusty stood again, stretched like a cat, started for the house.

Wait a minute, said Dwayne. Me and Mickey Dean had this idea about Bobby Lee's TV show, about getting our band to learn "Hey Good Lookin'" so we could audition to get on, you know. They have these auditions, and maybe we could take that dancing chicken along. That would probably help us get on the show.

That's a idea. I watch that show sometimes. You need to get some chickens, man.

Yeah. See you later.

See you.

Larry Lime walked toward the stopped train, deciding which cars to step between. His mama would have supper ready.

3

Uncle Young, on Mondays, late in the day, drove from Starke in a refrigerated truck to pick up fresh lungs, livers, stomachs, spleens, and hearts from a beef slaughterhouse in Flint Springs, North Carolina. The meat run. He delivered the animal parts in large vats to the dog food factory in Starke, where they were frozen before being ground up to be used in dog food—for protein.

Jared Fitzsimmons, the owner of the Barclay County Dog Food Factory in Starke, had recognized that cow lungs, livers, hearts, et cetera, were a cheaper protein than grains.

On this Monday, Larry Lime was riding along in the big truck, his first trip. He and Uncle Young talked about the marches, demonstrations, those things.

Some were happening as close as Summerlin and Durham.

There was this guy used to do stuff like that, said Uncle Young. Something Robinson. Singer.

Would you ever do a sit-in?

Naw. Uncle Young glanced over at the boy. But if them George Wallaces and them pasty power pigs keep running things, then it's going to get worse before it gets better. And they ain't gone convict none of them folks doing all that stuff. No such thing as a fair trial.

They passed big, open fields of freshly planted tobacco, soybeans, and corn. Barns, ponds, stretches of hardwood and pine.

Why wouldn't you do a sit-in? asked Larry Lime.

I wouldn't make any difference. And Fitzsimmons might find out. It's not my style. You think about going in the army, or the meat business. The man with the slaughterhouse where we going, he do all right. He do all right. You'll see. Uncle Young took a draw off his Pall Mall, put it back to the air vent. But ain't nobody gone get as rich as Fitzsimmons.

How'd he get so rich? asked Larry Lime.

Make money on everything he do. Now he saving money somehow by getting this meat from the slaughterhouse.

What do they do in there? Larry Lime knew how it

worked at "Lung River" once they got the entrails back to the dog food factory in Starke.

First, said Uncle Young, they gone zap the cow 'tween the eyes with a *stun* gun. It don't kill her because they want her to bleed right after they cut her throat with a razor big as a ball bat, right after these logging chains pull up her back legs so the blood drains out good, and then they get another big razor and split her open, and she moving on down the 'sembly line with the other cows, see, and you got a lung man cut out the lungs, throw them in a vat, and then a liver man, and so on. But they got to get ice on them parts right away, see, 'cause they about a hundred degrees when they come out, and they real pretty pink, but you ain' careful they start going a little blue, then a little green. *Watch* out, now. Them *lungs* can go green real quick. So they fill up vat after vat and then me and you roll the vats in the back of the truck. But we buy the ice by the pound, so we don't want too much of it melted, *seepage* what they call it, and I have to kind of look for that. And the more ice, the more water, and the more water, the more sloshing out you get.

What happens, Larry Lime asked, to all that stuff on the days we don't come get it?

Other people pick it up to make stuff women put on their faces. Soap people. Jell-O people. Cooking oil people. And so on. And they keep them great big old razors with big handles sharp enough to split a hair. And some of them great big razors got motors running them.

Uncle Young liked to tell in some detail because it was dramatic—and he'd memorized the telling of it.

Back in Starke after the meat run, Uncle Young backed the refrigerated truck up to "Lung River"—the storage room with a conveyor belt, which was next to the freezer room at the dog food factory.

Set up the ramp, Knothead, he said to Larry Lime.

He and Larry Lime rolled the vats out of the truck and into the room where six women from West Starke— including Larry Lime's mama, Canary Nolan—waited. The women tossed the organs into a revolving cement mixer that splattered ice on them before it shot the meat onto a conveyor belt that moved under running garden hoses. Then the women sorted, washed, and packed the meat parts into waxed cardboard boxes for freezing. The boxes were conveyed by carts into the freezer room.

The women worked part-time from nine p.m. until one a.m.

Hey, Mama, said Larry Lime.

Hey, Larry Lime, said Canary, looking over her shoulder while grabbing for a big, slick, black-red liver.

4

THE BACK WINDOWS of the furniture shop were usually open to relieve the building of paint-remover fumes. On most afternoons, late, the crows heard Larry Lime practice piano in the back room after work. Music phrases were played, repeated, repeated, repeated.

The crows could also hear the practice sessions of Dwayne and Mickey Dean's five-piece rock and roll band.

One crow, sitting out back, sometimes quietly mumbled a complaint about something, a human sound almost. Larry Lime had begun to get to know these crows, especially when he sat above the lowland and watched them—the lovely lowland where the plantation wagon path ran through the woods a hundred years before. In the smell of weeds and grasses, near where he sat looking down from the rise there at the curve in the footpath by the railroad track, where you could sit down on the suitcase-size rock and look down through the lowland—in the smell of those weeds and grasses, and in the feel of the air, would reside the elements, the forces that years later sparked Larry Lime's memory of the crows' movements and sounds. The lowland was their sanctuary, and that one crow with the white birthmark on the front of her wing would sometimes come close when Larry Lime threw corn bread from his pocket down the incline toward the bottom. He'd named her Coal. He'd noticed the way she carried herself and hopped—before he ever noticed that white marking. She had a tilt-left, tilt-right walk, like his hen Redbird.

The hard-packed footpaths between East and West Starke were walked mostly by people from Larry Lime's west side of the railroad, headed to or from work in homes of white people or the dog food factory, or to catch the Whittier–Prestonville bus or the school bus at the Bone Brick Store.

Staples—flour, sugar, coffee, salt, pepper, tobacco, snuff—were bought by people from both Starkes at the Bone Brick Store (chicken bones were visible here and there in the mortar). In both communities, garden vegetables were sometimes frozen in back-porch freezers, sometimes traded. So not many people found reason to drive all the way to Whittier to visit the supermarket. But the number of housewives who did make the drive was increasing from year to year.

The business of bartering was fading, as were small farms. According to influential economics professors from North Carolina State University, small farms were becoming "economically nonviable."

During summer, out from Starke, you'd see large fields of tobacco, and on toward fall, you'd see bodies in the fields "working in tobacco." Most of the youth in Starke and Prestonville, and some in Whittier, worked in tobacco in the summer. A majority of adults had done so growing up. Several tobacco warehouses operated in Prestonville, one in Starke, none in Whittier; and in those warehouses—in the twenties and thirties especially, slacking off some up through the sixties and seventies—acoustic blues music was performed during late-summer and fall tobacco sales. Some performers were legendary: Reverend Gary Davis, Big Clifton Simms, Sonny Terry and Brownie McGhee, Buster Suggins, Little Martha, Soup Can Carl, Peg Leg Sam, Denny Douglas, and others.

And down there in Prestonville—called West Preston by most blacks in the area—was a much larger black community than in West Starke, and there you could find barbershops, clothing shops, and restaurants. Larry Lime, his parents, and brother and sister all rode down there in their green '49 Plymouth after church two or three times a year to eat at their favorite restaurant, Lynette's.

Jobs for many men and women in Starke, Prestonville, and Whittier — white women worked in the home, generally, as did a few black women — were at Sears (white), selling cars in Whittier (white), as clerks in the black-run stores in Prestonville (black), selling insurance (white, one black), working at the hosiery mill in Prestonville (white), working as farm laborers (white, black), doing domestic work (black), refinishing furniture at Dwayne's daddy's store (white, black), working at Jared Fitzsimmons's dog food factory (white, black), and so on.

From the Bone Brick Store, southeast Starke, you traveled north about a quarter mile along Prestonville Road to Mr. Hallston's furniture-refinishing shop. And then on a bit north was the dog food factory, once a phosphate factory that Flash Acres's mama called the *fiss fott* factory. That place was bought by Jared Fitzsimmons in '54 and converted into the dog food factory. Starke Baptist Church and Starke School were on north a ways. And then just north of Starke was the Frog.

General Johnston had marched along Prestonville Road—north to south—less than a hundred years earlier on the way to fight Sherman and finally surrender near Durham.

Starke people didn't dwell on the Civil War—or on a lot else from the past—beyond family stories. They kept few diaries. Jared Fitzsimmons kept a kind of diary for recording the weather and meetings, but nothing about his feelings, sentiments, conversations. Some children at school kept journals because they were required.

Many people filled out family trees and birth and death dates in family Bibles. And more than you might think kept notes in the margins of family Bible flyleafs.

On Friday, after his second lesson with the Bleeder, Larry Lime walked home along the footpath that ran next to the swath of wooded lowland on his right. The church and, then, small-frame houses to his left.

Ahead of him, beyond Luther's Chin Road and other houses, lay the site of the now-gone Fitzsimmons' plantation. But the plantation's Half Mile Pond remained. A well-worn wagon path once extended from the plantation grounds straight to a small railroad loading station, but in the Civil War aftermath the plantation more or less broke down into a number of small farms, and that path vanished into an invisi-

ble center line in the woodland to Larry Lime's right—
the stretch of lowland that sometimes flooded, about
as wide as a football field. The plantation loading station at the railroad tracks had rotted, melded, disappeared into the ground and under vines in a slow-motion
sequence that took about a century.

Larry Lime could see the back of the church from
the path he walked. Lowland to his right, church to his
left. Liberty Day of Reckoning A.M.E. Church, also
named by Aunt Marzie. The church congregation
started growing a few years back with the arrival of
Reverend Alfonzo Manning and his wife, July Manning. Mrs. Manning brought vibrant new music that
attracted people from Whittier and Prestonville. She
had a beautiful voice. She introduced tambourines to
the choir. Some of the church people didn't like it, but
most did, and they all liked Brother Manning, a friend
of Martin Luther King Jr.

The white preacher at First Baptist in East Starke
was Ted Stephens, an interim preacher who'd been on
duty for a year while the search committee looked for a
new preacher. They found one, but he didn't work out
and the committee had called Ted back. So he was now
into his second year, and people liked him, some saying
he should stay on. Ted had secretly advised a group of
white students involved in the Greensboro sit-ins three

years before, though nobody in Starke knew that. He'd even met with negro ministers in Greensboro, becoming friends with one named Isaac Wilson. Once, in a conversation with Isaac Wilson, he confided that he was friends with an atheist. Ted never forgot what Isaac said: None of my people can afford to be atheists.

When Ted got "the call" from Starke, he had come, fit in, and spoke in the strongest voice he could muster about "the inspired word of God" and a "personal Jesus," though he didn't embrace those concepts. He even believed in racial integration and all that, and though he didn't believe in a literal heaven and hell, he didn't talk about those nonbeliefs because such talk would ensure the shutdown of his income from a relatively easy job, his comfortable social life, and lots of fried chicken. He was a bit overweight. And one reason for his popularity in the church was that once a month he visited every mama over seventy-five years old, twice a month for the shut-ins.

So Alfonzo Manning and Ted Stephens were Starke's tribal elders. A small Methodist Church, Mount Mission Methodist, south of Starke, used a circuit rider setup. No one preached there regularly.

The man holding formal power, through an obsessive interest in wealth, was Jared Fitzsimmons, owner of quite a few of the houses west and east of the tracks. He also owned the dog food factory, the TV station, and the white newspaper in Prestonville, the *Prestonville Courier-News* (named the *Caucasian-Leader* until 1954). The black newspaper in West Preston, run out of the back of a filling station, was the *Prestonian Mercury.*

Larry Lime approached the north–south dirt road, Luther's Chin Road. Just across it was his house—in a row of six. Two oaks and a persimmon tree stood in the front yard. In back was the chicken coop, the garden, and a garage with a small room attached—called "the smokehouse," though no smoke was involved. The four-room house was fronted by a porch, flyswatter hanging by the door.

Scrap, their little white and tan "sooner" dog, slept on the porch. He'd got to staying gone lately. Redbird, the dancing chicken, trotted toward Larry Lime as he pulled corn bread from his pocket. She looked like a happy, big-bosomed lady in a red dress, swaying side to side.

Larry Lime saw several chickens under the small front porch; he looked for the rooster. His daddy didn't want any more roosters for a few years. Three of the chickens were pets—Redbird, Snowball, and Minnie. Canary had named Minnie after Memphis Minnie. The nine or so others were just chickens.

Larry Lime walked around the house and across the packed-dirt backyard to the well house and slid back the heavy top. He reached in with a feed scooper and scooped chicken feed from the big bag, then walked to the pen and slung the feed along a chicken trough. Chicken wire covered the top of the pen. Minnie walked toward him from the side of the house.

When Redbird was just a chick and cooped up, Larry Lime would stick his finger through the wire. She's the only one that would allow him to run his fingertip over the beginnings of her comb.

Snowball would crouch the first time you walked up to her in the morning. And if you grabbed her and held her to the ground, she'd raise her tail feathers. Uncle Young said they thought they were about to get hosed. Said they'd open up back there, that a white man in Prestonville got took to court by his wife for hosing chickens. She told the judge he had sex with eleven pullets, and she brought one to court to show for evidence, and the last paragraph of the "In Brief" section of the *Prestonville Courier-News* said, "The chicken will be examined by the crime lab."

The following question/answer ran a few weeks later in the *Prestonian Mercury*, no introduction, no explanation:

Q: Why did the chicken cross the road?
A: To get out of Prestonville.

Larry Lime skipped up the three steps to the small back porch, entered the kitchen. To his right was a bedroom. Straight ahead was the living room—with a fireplace. Another bedroom was off the living room.

On summer nights, Larry Lime's mother, Canary, shut all the windows in the house except for one in each bedroom. A living room window fan, installed by Uncle Young, pulled in cool night air.

Booker gave Canary the window side of their bed, and on those nights when he was home, he'd sometimes lean over her so that he could breathe and whisper into her ear.

When Larry Lime came into the kitchen, Canary turned from the stove, a four-eyed electric. Was he there today? she said.

Yes, ma'am. He gone teach me sure enough.

Jazz might get him outen the South, she thought. It was a familiar thought for all her children—with other words for "jazz." She'd been stirring black-eyed peas. She was short, with a soft, round face.

Larry Lime sat at the kitchen table, picked up a piece of cold corn bread from a platter.

I got fresh corn bread on, said his mother. What's he gone charge you?

He ain't said nothing about that yet. Larry Lime took a bite of the cold corn bread, put it back.

Don't bite that then put it back.

Larry picked it up, took another bite, placed it on his plate.

But what about Mrs. Manning? said Canary.

She won't mind.

July Manning had taught Larry Lime what she taught all her piano pupils during their first lesson. Larry Lime couldn't hear her name without thinking about it: "Rain Is Falling Down." The notes were E–E (rain is) D–D (falling) C (down). E–E (rain is) D–D (falling) C (down). E–E (pitter) D–D (patter) E–E (pitter) D–D (patter). E–E (rain is) D–D (falling) C (down). Sitting at the piano beside Mrs. Manning, Larry Lime's heart sped up the first time he heard the melody because he knew he could play it. He memorized it after hearing it once through. Mrs. Manning, in the next months, worked him through two worn instruction books from the Thompson piano series. Soon after his first lessons, he was picking up songs by ear, playing hymns with one-note bass patterns.

And as Larry Lime took lessons, Canary often thought of the piano standing in the house in Whittier. She and her mother cleaned that house when she was a little girl. She wasn't allowed to touch the long, black piano, except for dusting.

She said, The Bleeder's name is Josh Aimes, I think. You ought to call him Mr. Aimes.

He just told me the Bleeder.

Well, it'll be all right if Uncle Young say it don't mess up the trash hauling. But you tell me if he want to charge you something.

Uncle Young say it's okay. He said I can walk home and he'll take the load to the dump.

We'll see. She walked to her and Booker's bedroom, opened the door. Supper, she said. At the back door, she blew a metal police whistle that she kept hanging from a nail by the screen. Her two youngest, Izzy and Bethany, came running for supper.

On the table she set a plate of fried fatback, a bowl of turnip greens, a bowl of black-eyed peas, and the plate of flat, fried corn bread pieces. A pitcher of tea and five glasses of ice cubes were already there.

Booker, pulling an overall strap over his shoulder, wandered in from the bedroom.

Larry Lime's brother and sister came in from the backyard, took a seat at the table.

Canary often visualized her children gone out of the South. She had two cousins in New York and two in Detroit. Her oldest son, Tinker, was staying with one in Detroit.

It didn't look like Larry Lime, influenced by his daddy and Uncle Young, would be a preacher. And he had a girlfriend Canary didn't trust. And then that awful, hounding Flash Acres, one of the worst of the crackers, was Larry Lime's foreman at the furniture shop. He seemed to soak up meanness, especially now that the movement had commenced. Reverend Manning knew Dr. King, some white people knew that, and word was that if Dr. King came to Hanson County, the Prestonville Klan would raise a ruckus. There was talk they'd burn down the church, bomb homes like they were doing in other places. Especially down in Alabama. They'd just arrested Dr. King down there. And that story in *Look* magazine somebody had at church, about that Till boy. Those men admitted they killed him—because he whistled at a white woman—and those men were free. If the boy had been white they'd just laughed at him, and now that that boy was dead, nothing, no government, no jury in Mississippi, no president, nobody, would do nothing about it, except God, in His own good time. And that was seeming mighty slow.

Say the blessing, Larry Lime, she said.

God is great, God is good, and we thank him for the sun for warmth, the moon for love, and for getting us up in the morning. Amen.

Canary started bowls around. She said to Booker, That man with the bleeding disease told Larry Lime he'd teach him some jazz piano.

Who's that? Booker glanced at Larry Lime. His voice was deep and full of sleep. He was a big man.

The Bleeder, said Larry Lime, looking up from his food.

The Bleeder? I heard of him. Booker spooned black-eyed peas onto his plate. You need to be learning to run a chain saw.

I can run a chain saw.

Who taught you that?

Uncle Young.

That's what do you some good.

Booker had lost his last job a month before — a construction job with Sargo Kerr in Summerlin, the biggest road builder in the state. Just afterward, he stood at the "work station" — a small rock formation — in front of the Bone Brick Store, where black men stood on weekends, sometimes weekdays. A white man would drive up, say Work? and then negotiate with the first man in line — the worker leaning in at the passenger window or standing back a ways from the driver's window, listening to what was expected for the day and what he'd be paid. Without approaching a car, Booker walked home, said, Never again.

5

JUNEBUG'S SKATING RINK, a wooden building built in 1936 by the WPA, stood in East Starke at the east end of the North Cut. Inside, the beadboard walls and ceiling were painted red and white. Large speakers blasted popular music: "Wake Up Little Susie," "Green Onions," "Maybellene." Every Friday and Saturday night the place was packed, also on some school-day afternoons when whole classes walked there through the woods from the school. On Monday night it was open to black people.

At the far end of the big parking lot behind the rink, white boys parked their cars after weekend movies in Whittier or Prestonville — or after Sunday night church services — to make out with their girlfriends.

Occasional fornication, but most of the action was heavy petting.

Black boys who drove cars parked behind the rink on Monday nights, but not on other nights. They had a place at the west end of the North Cut near their ball field.

Dwayne Hallston had been dating Linda Prentiss for four months. She was from down in Prestonville, a little house north of town on Prestonville Road. She was in the tenth grade. Dwayne was a junior.

He got his hands in her panties most Saturday nights and sometimes Sunday nights while they parked behind the skating rink. Six to eight cars were usually there on Saturday nights. Maybe three on Sunday nights. On most Sunday nights he took her to her church in Prestonville, Mount Zion Baptist, and after church he'd head again for the parking lot behind Junebug's. In the wide front seat of his daddy's white '60 Buick LeSabre, clear plastic seat covers, Dwayne would maneuver into a comfortable position on his back, no clothes taken off. Linda crawled up on him, fully dressed, bra unshackled. She just pumped and pumped, and he did too, both finally breathing like they'd run a mile. He could get off that way and was pretty sure she did as well. They could never bring themselves to mention it. But that didn't hold them back.

Dwayne, on this Saturday night, summer of '63, after a lusty session, car window open, that one flood-light shining from the corner of Junebug's, breeze on the sweat of his neck, faint smell of semen in the air, said to Linda, I been listening to horns a lot lately, you know, like in "The Jam, Part I." We're going to get two horn players from up in Whittier. Brothers. Darren and Gaston Dell. Somebody said they were dating the Caldwell sisters for a while. You know them?

I don't know any horn players, I don't think.

I was thinking you just might know them as people, not horn players. Regular people who dated Tina and Gina.

I remember there were some twins dating them, or maybe it was just brothers, but I never knew their names, I don't think.

It was probably them then. Once they start playing with us we can do a whole new kind of music. Rhythm and blues. Kind of, you know, like James Brown or some of them. A horn section makes a whole new sound.

Linda straightened her skirt. She asked, Did Mickey Dean date Judy Loy? Cindy was asking me about it.

I don't know. I don't think so.

Would you find out?

Sure. Me and Mickey Dean are going to do this thing with a chicken we can't tell nobody about yet.

You mean in the band?

Naw, at *The Birds*. The movie. We're going to drop a chicken out of the balcony when all those children start running down the hill and the birds are all pecking at their heads.

Dwayne looked out past Linda, into the woods, at a light way down through the trees. You ready to go? he said.

Yeah, let's hurry up. I want to see the last half of *Bobby Lee*.

Oh, yeah. Dwayne cranked the Buick. Maybe I'll watch a few minutes. Mama and Daddy have started staying up for it.

6

PEOPLE ON *BOTH* SIDES of the tracks enjoyed *The Brother Bobby Lee Reese Country Music Jamboree* (earlier called the *Country Music Jamboree* — and later called *The Bobby Lee Reese Show*), Saturday nights at ten thirty, live, right out of Hanson County's WLBT TV channel 7, down the road toward Prestonville.

Baby Mercy DeCoupe (Dey-coo) was Bobby Lee's on-air female sidekick. Jared Fitzsimmons, station owner, had asked Bobby Lee for good country music, clean humor now and then, and at least one gospel tune each Saturday night.

The sponsor of the show was Fitzsimmons's dog food business, Barclay County Dog Food (so named by a hired consultant).

Jared, a Little Jimmy Dickens fan, also liked Bill Monroe and the Bluegrass Boys, and Lester Flatt and Earl Scruggs. He told people that out of all his accomplishments, he was most proud of that show. He watched it every Saturday night and had had to hire more and more people to handle steadily increasing dog food sales.

The show had spread like wildfire and was now putting Hanson County on the North Carolina entertainment map. Fitzsimmons sold the show to one TV station after another. Radio stations played some episodes, especially those episodes with country music stars, and the extra funny ones with Bobby Lee. Rumors had it that the show was moving to Nashville or New York.

And you might wonder why descendants of slaves in rural North Carolina, 1963, tuned in to a country music show. For one thing, the only other TV show at ten thirty on Saturday nights was a thirty-minute weather program hosted by Gabe Ferguson, who kept dropping his map pointer. But it was also because of Bobby Lee Reese: his apparent naive generosity and his ability to talk to black people under the white radar. Aunt Marzie said, He talk about us all sand lugging and suckering out there in that hot sun. He gits it, and he ain't all wound up and worried up.

Roy Acuff sang on the third show back in late '59. Little Jimmy Dickens flew in from Nashville for the sixth show. Virginia Buysse came up from New Orleans with her Cajun accordian. Everybody involved in the early going at the station had the sense that the show would be a big hit. Not that Baby Mercy didn't add a lot — she was pretty and perky — but Bobby Lee Reese was the main reason people tuned in. Most of the older folks raised on the farm — long asleep by ten thirty p.m. — didn't tune in, but middle-aged and young people did.

Bobby Lee, who moved with his parents to Summerlin, North Carolina, from Medina, Ohio, at age eleven and went on to get a history degree from Ballard College in Summerlin, realized that his main TV audience in eastern and southeastern North Carolina and northern South Carolina would be a people with not all that much written history, a people who didn't seem very interested in history even. Bobby Lee's study of the Fitzsimmons plantation, what history he could track down, had been the subject of his honor's thesis. While gathering interviews, he found out how little most residents knew about the place.

He moved back to Ohio after graduating from Ballard, and then, after a marriage and divorce, moved back south to Whittier, and from there answered the audition call for MC on the *Country Music Jamboree*.

Bobby Lee knew his audience was verbal, not in a big-vocabulary way, but in an unconsciously artful way. And this is one of the reasons he'd moved back from Ohio. He missed the talk.

He soon found the key to holding a big audience and building a bigger one: telling family stories. After all, during his years in North Carolina he'd adopted the accent and could use it when he pleased. He also decided he'd do something silly on the show: *eat dog food.*

He had no idea that that simple, outlandish act would draw such a viewing crowd.

At first he hadn't counted on a black audience, but that audience did come on, if slowly. So he studied, carefully building up a stash of words, phrases, exclamations, movements, stances, looks pulled from intersections of black and white language, food, and norms. He planned and cataloged with Baby Mercy, who helped him work out a simple formula. He would spend a good bit of time in front of the camera, alone, wearing a straw farmer hat. He'd laugh hard at his own stories—like Red Skelton. He'd put his hand on his thigh, just above the knee, and bend over laughing. This part wasn't planned exactly—Bobby Lee's laughter at his own stuff was genuine.

He started finding his own niche—the funny family stories. Baby Mercy was providing many of them. She'd walk up to him while he was on camera and ask the leading questions, and sometimes he'd get on a roll and ad-lib about a character he'd introduced a month or two before.

7

April 18, 2011

RAY WHEELER, former piano player for Dwayne's rock and roll band, drives from Atlanta to Rosehaven Convalescent Center in Summerlin, North Carolina, to interview Bobby Lee Reese. Ray, a retired lawyer, is researching an article he's writing for the music issue of *Oxford American* magazine. The piece will be called "A Short History of *The Bobby Lee Reese Show*." From the interview:

BOBBY LEE REESE: *Jared Fitzsimmons found out about Baby Mercy, who fronted a band over in Meat Camp, not that far away. Not the Meat Camp in the mountains. There were two Meat Camps in North Carolina back then, but the second got merged into* the town they named Hilltop: There was Meat Camp, Dodger, and Stumpy Point. They were close together, and business people wanted them combined under a new name. They should have left the names alone. Did you know about that?

RAY WHEELER: *Yeah, I heard about that. All within about a three-mile radius. Like Fuquay-Varina and Eden.*

BOBBY LEE REESE: *Anyway, Jared showed me a picture from the newspaper of Baby Mercy with her band. That was a Sunday night, and on Tuesday morning he introduced us in his office, and in two weeks we had our first show together. Did you know Jared, by the way?*

RAY WHEELER: *Just knew of him, mainly. I saw him a few times.*

BOBBY LEE REESE: *Strange man. But I'm the one seemed kind of strange around there back then. I guess I was one of the first men around that part of the country wearing a visible gold necklace — and Baby Mercy kind of liked jangly jewelry offstage, and*

I don't know if this had anything to do with it, though it's something I remember, and most people didn't know, but what happened was we fell in love. We kept it private though. Figured for some reason that that would be best for the show. And it was fun keeping it a secret. She was not the shy type, but, you know, she always seemed interested in whoever — or whomever — she was talking to, a kind of interest that you wouldn't expect from somebody as attractive as she was. She dressed a bit on the gaudy side, in my view, but one minute into a five-minute conversation with her and you would not fault her one iota because . . . what dominated the room she was in would be her eyes, bedroom *eyes, very green, with that thick red hair, and freckles. And her hair was not a light, bright red, but a deep red, dark. She wore the blond wig for the show, you remember, and the white cowboy hat.*

We'd sit in my little house over there on Maycross Road, about a mile north of the Frog, this place where you could hear good jazz. A guy, a black guy called the Bleeder, played there some. Baby Mercy would have her car in my garage with the garage door closed, and we'd sit in the living room on my sofa and I'd write down ideas for stories to tell on the show.

She came from a sure-enough backwoods family in East Tennessee, seven brothers and sisters, and she loved to cook pies. Her specialty was rhubarb pie, and of course she did the staples — apple, peach, cherry.

I was not inclined to put on weight back then. I could eat anything I wanted, you know. Anyway, me and Baby Mercy would sit there in my living room, thinking up ideas and rehearsing, and I'd be eating pie. She loved to make me laugh, sitting there on the couch — me taking notes — asking her about her family and all. She'd go home to Tennessee and come back with new stories about her folks, and I'd adapt them for the show, use them over and over with a little change or twist here and there, same names.

See, the secret was that people tell the same family stories over and over — you know that — and if it wasn't your own family then they'd get old, but if it was your family, then the story had a special meaning — like seeing something precious over and over. Something you couldn't exactly touch, but something you could look at over and over. In a box. Open it up over and over, you know what I mean?

RAY WHEELER: *My family didn't tell stories much, but my wife's did...does. Tell me a little more about the job.*

BOBBY LEE REESE: *Well, my job was to make the people in the audience feel like I was talking about their families — not somebody else's. So I made up a few aunts' and uncles' and cousins' names, and those were the only ones I talked about. And I was surprised early on to have black people come up and say, "Hey, you're the one on that show that eats the dog food." And then maybe say something about the stories too. I was surprised, except maybe I shouldn't have been. So I started getting as much southern flavor into the stories as possible, you know, including everybody. I worked at it. I studied it.*

We laughed our asses off sitting there on the couch, Baby Mercy and me — I — and we came up with the dog food eating idea early on — after about a year, I think — and that's when the show took off for sure.

8

May 1963

Flash Acres's mama — in the face — looked like a mole wearing glasses. Her two front teeth rode her lower lip, and the glasses were thick and round. She lived across the street from the Bone Brick Store with her thirty-three-year-old son, Flash. She was crazy about Bobby Lee's TV show. Excited that Flash was going to audition for it.

She was happy Flash was a furniture shop foreman, had a job close to home working for Marcus Hallston, Dwayne's daddy. Mr. Hallston and Flash's Mama were first cousins, and the two families all got together at Dwayne's house for Sunday dinner every couple of months or so. Dwayne's mama, Swansee, had learned to get along with Flash's mama pretty well.

Flash's Mama had never been all that happy that Flash had taken two extra years to get through school, failing once in sixth grade, "held back" as the principal put it, failing again in the eleventh grade because of that English teacher with the black-rimmed glasses and crossed eyes who looked like she walked with a brick up her rear end. Lord, couldn't *nobody* talk to *her.* In that particular case, Flash's Mama set up an appointment, went and sat down in the principal's office, and announced to both teacher and principal that if she herself couldn't by God understand a homework assignment, then how in the Good Lord's name was her son supposed to understand it? Would the principal read the assignment out loud and explain it to her? Well, get this, the principal sat there like a knot on a stump, refusing to read it out loud, and he would *not* explain the assignment to her, so Flash's Mama concluded right then — and later told anybody who would listen — that the reason for the principal's silence was that he didn't understand the dern assignment his own dern self.

Flash's Mama wasn't exactly happy either that Flash was thirty-three years old without a regular girlfriend. Take that back. He had a girlfriend of sorts, but she wasn't regular and she seemed a lot more like just a friend. And besides that, she was not pretty, even though pretty is as pretty does. But Flash's Mama tried not to think about that so much yet, or worry about it. That department should work out okay, she figured. "All good things come to those who wait."

Over a supper of tomato sandwiches—mayonnaise, salt and pepper, and tomato slices on white bread—navy beans, and biscuits, Flash's Mama was talking about the colored boy who worked at the furniture shop. She asked Flash, If you don't know how much he makes, how do you know he don't make as much as you? She pictured pickaninnies from across the tracks wearing tow sacks with head and arm holes. She'd seen that with her own two eyes—those Nolans with the funny names, like Sammy My Good God Almighty Nolan. All of them birthed and named by Aunt Marzie. Why, one of them was named something-something Seaboard Air Line Railroad Kitchen Nolan because he'd been born in the kitchen when the dern night train was coming through.

'Cause I'm the foreman, Mama, said Flash. Marcus ain't gone pay Larry Lime-Pass-the-Time as much as me. And Larry Lime-Pass-the-Time is sitting on the wall out there at the store like him sitting on the wall is okay. Like them boys at the lunch counter up in Summerlin. And nobody cares.

Ain't his mama one of them works at the dog food factory?

The "Lung River" part. Yes. Freezing the meat.

I wonder what Jared Fitzsimmons pays her?

I'm happy where I'm at.

Well, I won't suggesting you go to work over there, son.

Flash looked at his sandwich. Part of his tomato was coming out. This tomato won't peeled, he said.

I know that. And I'm getting tired of them creeping into things and places they ain't got no business.

Flash looked up. *Tomatoes?*

No. Like that Nat King Cole for goodness' sakes, hair slicked back like a greased pig, and that big eat-the-cat grin, and them saying things and showing their fannies all over, and those boys sitting at that lunch counter in Greensboro and Summerlin, and not one white man in the whole town with gumption to throw their black asses out on the sidewalk. Your daddy would have.

She had never mentioned to Flash his daddy's membership in the KKK, but she knew about it, took comfort that Flash might join himself. She'd found a notice about a meeting among his things.

She worried a little bit because in addition to him

not being interested in girls all that much, he sulked in his room more than he ought to. He *was* talented in music, sang and played country music—especially Ernest Tubb—on the guitar his daddy left him, a Kay brand from Sears. A kind of small guitar. Some really big things could come out of that audition for the TV show.

Saturday night at about eight thirty she went to Flash's bedroom door and said, Will you help me wash my hair before Bobby Lee comes on?

I might.

Flash is trying to be funny, she figured. Standing there in her housecoat and pink slippers, head lowered, she wondered whether or not to say anything else. She turned and walked to the kitchen. She'd eat a couple of cookies, drink some milk, and later on watch *I Love Lucy* and then *Amos 'n' Andy*. Now *that* was one funny show. Somebody said the actors were really white, but they sure looked and sounded like colored people to Flash's Mama.

She'd recently had a cataract operation and wasn't supposed to bend over. She usually washed her hair in the kitchen sink on Saturday nights, but now that she couldn't bend over, Flash had to help out.

At the last commercial of *I Love Lucy*, Flash's Mama stood from the couch and walked to the bathroom, filled her water glass, took out her upper and lower dental bridges, and dropped them in the water.

When she returned, Flash was sitting in jeans and a white T-shirt in his chair. It was so good to have him at home evenings during the week, to cut the grass and take out the garbage and talk to, and on Saturday nights help her wash her hair.

Let's go ahead and wash my hair, she said. I hate to ask, but it won't my idea to have a catarack operation.

She pulled a chair to the sink, positioned it facing away from the sink, sat down, and leaned back with her neck against the lip of the sink, her hair under the faucet. Flash turned the faucet to the side, got the water warm. He rinsed her hair, washed it, scrubbing with the tips of his fingers while she held a dry washrag over her eyes.

Flash's Mama thought about his hands and what he could do: refinish furniture, play a guitar, fix things around the house that a lot of people who'd gone to college couldn't do. She wouldn't mind if he went ahead and got married, but that of course was entirely up to him.

It was good to think that if she got disabled for some reason she'd have him to live with — if she could get around. If she got real bad off she could always go to the County Home.

The way Flash dealt with his feelings for women was to say to himself that his mama was all the woman he could deal with for a while. And about men, he thought that he was the type of guy who could be a fast friend to any man — that's what he was capable of, fast friendship, when the right man came along. Flash knew he could never be a queer, that if he got too close to a man in friendship, then that man might try to play around with him in some strange way, and he didn't want any of that stuff, he supposed. So that's where he was at this point in his life — kind of waiting until his mama got put in the County Home or until she died, and then at that time he could take on the whole subject of womanhood in such a way that he would be able to find a wife, or if that failed, a room-mate, or hell, if need be, just live on into middle age like Tiny Roberts did, with his little trailer behind the church — him being the only white janitor that Flash had ever heard of. That seemed like an easy life, living in a trailer by himself.

Ladies and gentlemen, now straight from Sloppy Holler, just around the bend, please welcome Mr. Bobby Lee Reese...

...and Aunt Dormalee, said Bobby Lee, used to, you know, go to the grave cleaning over in Pitch Fork every spring, and of course Uncle Snog would come along too. So Uncle Snog started slowing down one year, couldn't do as much, you know, and then—the grave cleaning was always the first Saturday in May—the next year, and the year after that, Uncle Snog could only stand and rake for a minute or two, and then the *next* year he had to sit the whole time, but he did try to stand and do a little raking in his walker. The year after that he sat in his fold-up lawn chair the whole time. Next winter, before the *next* grave cleaning, he died.

Most of us went to the funeral, including Aunt Dormalee. So next spring, on the way to the grave-yard cleaning, we're riding along in the car with Aunt Dormalee and Aunt Leotie in the backseat, and Aunt Dormalee with her memory slipping a little says, "Well, I don't guess poor old Snog will make it to the grave cleaning this year."

And Aunt Leotie says, "Well, I *hope* not, Dorma-lee. For gracious' sakes."

Bobby Lee got all the pauses just right and turned to look at Baby Mercy off camera. He reached his right hand toward her, and she stepped on camera to intro-duce the next act. The amateur act.

Flash's Mama sat in the chair beside the couch, Flash on the couch, his hair still damp from his shower. She'd dried hers with a hair dryer.

I bet they pick you at that audition, she said. She had a quick thought — him famous and moving away. Here comes Baby Mercy, she said.

Baby Mercy, in her short dress with fringe and a white cowboy hat, walked onstage, stood in front of the band. The men in the band wore cowboy hats too. Ladies and gentlemen, she said, please welcome our amateur act for the week, the Gospel Joytunes doing "Spend a Little Time with Jesus."

At Larry Lime's house:

Aunt Marzie had walked from her house to watch *Amos 'n' Andy*. She was leaving now, just before Bobby Lee came on. The door was open and the night was warm. Larry Lime sat on the floor in front of the TV, blue-gray light reflecting from the walls. His brother and sister were in bed. Canary knitted and watched TV from the couch. Booker had a weekend job with a cousin in Prestonville. He'd be home after church tomorrow.

On *Amos 'n' Andy*, Andy had been sitting behind the controls of an airplane while showing off for a girlfriend who sat beside him. He thought the airplane was tied to the ground but it had accidentally taken off and was flying around. Andy thought it was still tied down, and he kept saying to his girlfriend, Why, I just fly the beam, honey. I just fly the beam.

Larry Lime thought about the show from the week before, the one where Kingfish found out that his old friend from high school had a maid. It wasn't as funny, but it showed rich colored people. A family in Prestonville was like that, he'd heard.

You need to stay and watch this, Canary said to Aunt Marzie, who was about to push open the screen door. Watch this man eat dog food. You ain't heard about him?

I have, but I ain't spending no time watching no white man eat dog food. She turned back and said, Next thing you know he be barkin', and then he be peeing on a tree.

You hear about the blind man, and his seeing eye dog peeing on his leg? asked Canary.

I have, said Aunt Marzie.

Larry Lime turned from the TV to his mama. What's that? he said.

Blind man standing on the corner, said Aunt Marzie, with his seeing eye dog peeing on the man's leg, and the man trying to feed him something when there was this—

It was a Fig Newton he was trying to feed him, said Canary.

Don't make no difference, said Aunt Marzie.

Yes it do. I'll tell it.

Then I'm going home. She pushed open the screen door.

Bye.

Bye, said Aunt Marzie, and left.

What was it? said Larry Lime.

Well, the blind man's seeing eye dog was peeing on his leg and the man was trying to feed the dog a Fig Newton, and a man standing across the street seen it and walked over and said, "Excuse me, sir, did you know your dog's peeing on your leg?" And the blind man said, "I sho did." And the man say, "Well, how come you trying to feed him a Fig Newton?" And the blind man say, "Soon's I find his head, I'm gone kick his ass."

Larry Lime laughed, looked at the TV, looked back at his mama, and said, I didn't know you'd tell no dirty joke.

It's a white man's joke.

Why you say that?

Whoever seen a black man with a seeing eye dog?

Larry Lime and his mother watched as the main man, the dog food eater, got introduced by the pretty woman and came on and starting telling a story about Uncle Cousin and his dog eating okra and a man with white shoes. Everybody laughed, then these singers came on. Larry Lime listened for chord changes. The

Bleeder had taught him—with the chords numbered. Most of the time the chord changes were like his mother's Little Walter records: one, four, five, occasionally a two, once in a while a three, sometimes a six. But there were strange ones too.

Larry Lime wondered if it was real dog food the man ate. The man was kind of like Uncle Young sometimes.

Somebody said white people didn't move in church, and he'd been outside Starke Baptist on a couple of Wednesday nights and heard the slow, sad singing, songs without any slang and curve, all square and tucked in at the corners. But they come up with these good movies like *Lawrence of Arabia*, and *The Birds*, and *Psycho*. And some of them played some pretty good music. The Bleeder would say, He white, but he swings.

This one, this white one, was back on, eating dog food, tossing it up a nugget at a time, catching it in a tin funnel he was holding in his mouth, and then he said something about eating it one piece at a time, and then he stopped, swallowed, and said:

My Aunt Dormalee never ate more'n one dog food nugget at a time when she was teaching me to eat it, and as far as Aunt Dormalee is concerned, big companies wouldn't be needed to produce things like paper towels, for one example, because Aunt Dormalee, right now, today, is using just one paper towel and one paper towel only, and that's the one she's been using since 1961 when the one she'd *been* using since 1958 just disappeared into thin air. She's bought just one roll of paper towels in her lifetime, and she's got the rest of that roll willed to Cousin Teresa. And she, by golly, when she finishes using ice, now listen to this, when she finishes using ice, she washes it off and sticks it right back in the freezer where ice belongs, and she keeps using the same ice cubes over and over while it gets littler and littler until it finally disappears. Poof. Now just think of all the electricity she saves by not having to freeze new ice.

Larry Lime, blue light on his face, said, That sounds like Aunt Marzie and her ice. That's exactly what she do.

Did I say Teresa? said Bobby Lee. Y'all remember Cousin Teresa. She's the one told me about my broke arm while I was sitting on the front-porch steps, waiting for mama to find a car to take me to the emergency room in, and my arm crooked as a broke pencil. She's the one stood there while I was bawling, both of us six years old, and she said, bending down with her hands on her knees, looking me in the eyes, she said, real quiet and serious like, "They might have to cut it off."

At Flash's house, Flash thought about how this TV show was something he and his mama had in common.

He couldn't go to church. Couldn't stand it. But him and his mama had this show and some food things they could talk about, and she was his mama.

He's as funny as Red Skelton, said Flash's Mama.

Yeah. Flash wished she'd ask him some more about the audition — what he was going to sing and all. What he might wear.

Bobby Lee had on his knee boots and overalls and straw hat — not exactly a cowboy hat — with curly hair coming out from under it.

That dog loved to eat okra, said Bobby Lee. And they buried him in the garden. Right underneath some okra plants. Dog went by the name of Boone. Y'all remember Boone. Ole Boone. Slobbered a lot. The very next year that okra bloomed prettier than ever. Okra blossoms. One of the most beautiful and under-rated flowers in the world. Cousin Spinny Mae had a okra blossom wedding bouquet when she married that used-car salesman who had a pair of shoes for every day of the week. That's the only way he could keep up with what day it was. When he got to his white shoes, he knew it was Sunday, and that's the *truth*.

Fifty miles away, a woman sitting on the couch in the living room of a new brick ranch house off a dirt road, a garden on one side of the house, said to her husband,

I bet he's got something in that bag asides dog food. At least on top. Some kind of cereal, something like that.

In his house trailer, northern Whittier, the Bleeder, alone, leaning back in a chair, his feet up on a table, reading a Chester Himes novel, listened to Thelonious Monk on his record player. Bobby Lee Reese was on TV. The sound was off.

Bobby Lee walked to a bag of dog food.

The Bleeder stood, walked to the TV, turned up the volume. I can't believe this, he said.

9

The Rumblers were:
Dwayne Hallston, trombone, rhythm guitar.
Mickey Dean Burgess, lead guitar, vocals.
Willy Wilson, electric bass.
Donnie Howell, drums.
Ray Wheeler, piano.

Their repertoire:
"Memphis," "Tequila," "Last Night," "Kansas City," "Mr. Blue," "Green Onions," "You Can't Sit Down." With the addition of Ray Wheeler on piano, they'd added "Forever," "Last Date," "Flip, Flop, and Fly."

They started planning for places to perform. Mickey Dean decided that when they learned three more songs they'd be ready. Somebody told him that thirteen songs was an hour's worth of performing. Their first gig would be at the Youth Center where they could do a one-hour set. And then they could play the July 4 picnic at the American Legion. Mickey Dean's granddaddy had already lined that one up. After they got four hours' worth of songs, they could start playing fraternity parties in Whittier. They figured that would happen by the end of the year.

Down behind Junebug's, Dwayne, sweaty, with Linda's head on his chest, talked about the band. So far all the songs are instrumental, he said, except for "Kansas City," "Flip, Flop, and Fly," and "Mr. Blue," and Mickey Dean wants to sing "Peanut Butter." He can do that real high voice.

Falsetto.

What?

That's what it's called. Falsetto. When something's up real high. Did he date Judy Loy?

Why?

You said you were going to find out.

I forgot to ask him. I don't think he did.

I want to know.

Why?

Because Cindy wants to know.

I don't know. I was talking about the band.

I was talking about Judy a month ago and you said you'd find out. Linda shifted and sat up straight in her seat.

I'll ask him. With the horns we can start learning all kinds of stuff that's kind of rhythm and blues. That'll get us a bunch of gigs, especially in fraternity houses. That's what Mickey Dean said.

Why don't you all do some country songs?

Naw, I don't think so. Except maybe some like Ray Charles is doing.

Canary was getting ready for bed. She'd been cooking. She cooked big on the second Saturday night of every month for next day's Sunday dinner at Uncle Young's, two o'clock, after church—sometimes two thirty— with Aunt Marzie attending.

Canary kept up with her family's meat—mostly sausage in tight cloth bags and salted hams hanging out back in the smokehouse. Uncle Young kept a few pigs belonging to him and Larry Lime's father. Uncle Young had a real smokehouse in his backyard.

The next morning, the second Sunday in May, Canary, Larry Lime, and his little brother and sister walked home from church in their Sunday clothes, up onto the front porch where Booker waited in an armless white undershirt and overalls.

He stood when he saw them coming, walked inside, put on his brown pleated dress pants and the yellow dress shirt Canary disliked. He had one yellow and one white dress shirt, three work shirts, two pairs of overalls, two pairs of work pants, and the dress pants.

When Booker walked out from the bedroom into the kitchen, Canary said, Booker, please don't wear that shirt.

Why come?

It look like mustard.

So?

It's ugly.

I like this shirt.

I wish you wouldn't wear it.

Other times, Booker went back to the bedroom, placed the shirt on a wire hanger and back into their small closet—so narrow that the hanging clothes were turned at an angle—and put on his white shirt. But sometimes, like today, he didn't pay Canary any mind. He said, I'm wearing it.

Larry Lime, along with his brother, sister, and parents, walked to Uncle Young's house, about a hundred yards north on Luther's Chin Road, and there, Aunt Marzie held court for a while with stories from way,

way back. Larry Lime and the adults—including two cousins and the preacher and his wife, Alfonzo and July Manning—sat at the long table in the dining room, a room that Uncle Young had added on with lumber from a house he'd helped tear down for Jared Fitzsimmons. The children, five of them, sat at the kitchen table. Before everybody started talking to everybody else, Aunt Marzie could get in a story or two. Today she was doing a little more explaining than normal for the benefit of the preacher and his wife. She had invited them.

Chucky Benjamin, Aunt Marzie explained, was the mayor's special assistant. He was our cousin. Chucky, she said, ran the courthouse up in Whittier and took care of all the colored peoples that was in trouble with the law. That was more attention than a lot of them get now, and he was a big, tall man, they said. This was right after Sherman come through, and victory was the Lord's. He was able to get a lawyer for the mens in jail, she said, and that was something that hadn't ever happened before then, or much since. And *his* mama was the one lost her children on a slave ship and then years later was separated up from her husband.

And then, she said, there was ole Mr. Yarborough, white man. He was some kin to the Fitzsimmons people. He sitting out there in the wagon path up the side of the plantation, sitting in a circle with all them rebels they

done captured, and he the one done bad things to her—
Chucky's mama I'm talking about—and she put a iron
kettle of water in the fireplace and just stood there waiting, and when it was bubbling like a rocky creek, she got
the hot pads and marched out with that pot and poured
that boiling water on that man's head and said, "I hope
you die in a Yankee jail, you no-good tub of guts," and
them Yankee soldiers just look at her and didn't do nothing except give her some hams from Mr. Yarborough's
own smokehouse itself, and that's the truth. And that
man's hair fell out. Some of it right there on the spot.
Like scalding a chicken. But then in the next years, bad
things started happening again, but…there was a few
years of sunshine when good things happened. Just a
very few years. Them were the years of happy deliverance, Mr. Manning.

And I think those days are coming again, said Reverend Manning. Don't you, Mama? he said to Mrs.
Manning.

I do, she said.

Chucky's wife, said Aunt Marzie, is the one started
the long names business when she give one to her son.
Her name was Aunt Flo.

And do you recall what that first long name was,
Mrs. Jones? asked Reverend Manning, appreciating
his own ability to be the straight man.

70

I sure do. Sunshine Booming Out of Darkness and Sorrow Benjamin. And they call him Sunny Boom Ben. What I heard. Could somebody pass me that chicken? I don't need no more'n a wing.

People from both sides of the track in Starke ate about the same amount — per capita — of corn bread, chicken, vegetables, pork, pies, cakes, stews. More chitterlings on the west side. About even on chicken necks, per capita.

You could hear "Pass me that corn bread" from one house.

"Mama, can I have the snap beans?" — from another.

"One more piece of fatback."

"Give me some butterbeans, please."

"That's good fried chicken. Pass me a leg."

"What, ain't but two biscuit left?"

"What happened to the biscuits?"

We could accurately say that the railroad divided a community of corn bread, vegetable, and chicken eaters; or a community of pet lovers; or a community of rural dialects; of families with men who hunted quail and rabbits; people who owned chickens; women who cooked and sewed; or people who had, in their lifetimes, "worked in tobacco" — picked it, carted it behind mule or tractor, tied it to sticks, hung it in barns to cure, took it to the market, complained about suckering and sand lugging.

And since about the same percentage of people called themselves Christian on both sides of the track, we *could* say that the railroad track divided a single Christian community. But something begins to break down there, doesn't it? The truths of their pasts gave each group a different God (one of deliverance, the other of dominion), a different mode of worship service (one with energy and joy trumping solemnity and fear, the other almost reversing that). And their histories brought hardships to the people of West Starke not understood by the people of East Starke, and guilt to the East not understood by anybody—a guilt that if moving deep in a lake, would leave the surface flat calm.

On that May Sunday night—as light began to evaporate at dusk and tall pines around the Liberty Day Church breathed without moving, as you heard the laughing and talking inside before the singing—the crows flew in and lit silently in the pines and oaks that stood between the church and the railroad tracks. They sat for a while and then flopped away unhurriedly, as below them a man with a gold chain around his neck and a redheaded woman, in the last darting of the sun's rays, walked to a spot on the tracks just up the incline from the church. They sat, listened to the music.

10

IN THE BACK ROOM of the furniture-refinishing shop, the large front panel of the old upright piano, hinged at top, was propped open on the back of Larry Lime's shoulders and head. I'm fixin' this note, he said to Dwayne, who'd come over to watch. Larry Lime looked around to be sure it was Dwayne. Together, they'd been working on a dresser in the big room, and Flash was gone. See, that right there goes right there, but it ain't pushing up against this down here because that's backed off. See that? That's how that note works.

Larry Lime and Dwayne were supposed to be working late on a big refinishing order from Jared Fitzsimmons, and Dwayne's daddy and Flash were driving to Clinton in the truck for two more dressers.

If they drive up, we got to get back in there, said Dwayne.

I know.

Dwayne noticed a Blue Horse notebook on the floor, open to a drawing of one note's internal hammer and mechanical parts. He leaned in to better see inside the piano.

This the one, said Larry Lime, you slide off it to hit that E, see? E-flat. It don't make no noise. Can you get me some of that glue from the tool chest? I can get the padding off that low note where don't nobody play and glue it on right here, see, right there. I'm having to play way up here. Larry Lime played a melody, right hand only, up high.

What's that?

What?

That tune.

"Swingin' Shepherd Blues," said Larry Lime. Can you get me that glue?

Walking to the tool chest, Dwayne thought about what he was doing. He certainly wouldn't do something for Larry Lime in front of Flash.

When Dwayne got back with the glue, he asked Larry Lime, Who showed you that song?

The Bleeder. Larry placed his right hand on the keyboard, played a chord. And then there's this. Another chord. Hear that. Each one got a different color. He showed me that too. Can you hear the different colors?

What color was that first one?

Kind of, I don't know, dark red, and the second one had some yellow in it, but it's something you hear, so it's a sound color. It has a feeling. So you got this, for example. He played. That's real square and marchy.

Play that "Swingin' Shepherd Blues" again, said Dwayne.

The Bleeder say it's a jazz tune that made the pop charts, said Larry Lime. This here where it slide off. It just slide off onto that. See? Onto that E. Hear that? That's why I got to fix this one.

Let me do that, said Dwayne. He played the grace note, then the E. Oh, yeah. Okay. But what about when you do this? End up on that B-flat. Is that called something? Because it —

That's a seventh, man. B-flat. That's the seventh. The big seventh, man. That take you by the hand and lead you right into the F chord, right there. Right into that number four chord. That's the move, man. That's the move. And look at this.

Larry Lime showed Dwayne a two-note piano chord: B-flat below middle C and the E-flat above middle C. A low C bass note at bottom.

This little riff, said Larry Lime. Listen. It's from the

Live at the Apollo album—slowed down, *do-do do-do do-do do-do*—that came before the two-note chord.

Dwayne realized he was experiencing a knowledge he didn't have. Who showed you that? he asked.

The Bleeder.

Live at the Apollo?

The new James Brown album. That riff stuck in between some of the songs. It's called "Hold It." 'Cept nobody but the Bleeder knows that. He likes James Brown, can play that stuff. It don't say "Hold It" on the album. See, like this. You play this: *do-do do-do do-do do-do*. And then the chord: *dat dat-dat dat*. Real fast. See? Listen. And as he played it, Larry Lime glanced at Dwayne, saw that he was caught up in it.

To Dwayne the sound was dirty and powerful and clean.

Larry Lime snapped his fingers, both hands—a little *ba-da ba-bap bap* syncopation. And, said Larry Lime, I'm going to see James Brown a week from Saturday night, man.

Where?

Summerlin, at the Big Center Auditorium.

Dwayne had a notion to tell Larry Lime that maybe he'd go too. White people did go, a few, and sat in the balcony. He'd heard of that. Mickey Dean would want to go. He and Mickey Dean could drive together, maybe see Larry Lime there, down below on the main floor.

I know he's got them horns, said Dwayne. And now we got these brothers, Gaston and Darren, in the Rumblers playing sax and trumpet. They sound good too, man. They harmonize. One of them writes out the parts.

That name, the Rumblers, said Larry Lime. That's kind of… Why don't y'all be named the *Amazing* Rumblers? I might want to go hear the *Amazing* Rumblers, but I don't think I'd go hear no Rumblers.

The Amazing Rumblers, said Dwayne. That does sound pretty good. Yeah.

You-all ought to learn some of them country songs and take Redbird on the TV station so she could dance. A fast country song. I got her dancing on a round, flat pan. I told you. All you got to do is put down the pan and she be right on that thing scratching away. You sing and it looks like she dancing to the singing.

How'd you teach her that?

Psychology stuff in a textbook—behavior conditioning or something like that—I just worked it so she didn't get no food unless she finally standing on the pan, scratching.

You think she'll do it for me?

Oh, yeah. Practice a couple of times with the band

so she get used to the noise. Then you can take her up to that TV audition.

Did you know Flash is going to audition? asked Dwayne.

To be on that show?

Oh, yeah.

Man, he got more nerve than he sound like he should. I heard him.

Somebody came in the door in the big room, the other room. Dwayne stepped to the doorway. It was his mother. She'd brought supper on a tray out to the shop for the two of them. On each paper plate: a pork chop, mashed potatoes, string beans, fried okra, corn bread, vinegar pickles. Paper cups of iced tea. She set the tray down on a table in the big room. Come get it, boys, she said.

Larry Lime's opinion, so far, was that Dwayne's mama was a good woman — not safe, necessarily. He'd figured her gentleness helped explain Dwayne not being uppity. But they both were out of reach, up there on whatever it was they stood on.

Larry Lime sat on a sawhorse in the big room, paper plate on a table. He eyed the okra, turning over a piece with his fork.

Dwayne's mother went into the back room, looking for something.

Larry Lime asked Dwayne, What your mama put on this okra?

Dwayne sat on the floor, cross-legged, holding his paper plate, eating. Salt, I reckon.

No, not after she fry it—before she fry it.

Dwayne's mama was coming out of the back room with a cardboard box.

What do you put on the okra, Mama, before you fry it?

I put a little bit of flour on there. Why?

Because Larry Lime said he bet his mama made better fried okra than you do.

I did not, said Larry Lime. He thought, *You crazy.*

Well, maybe she does, said Dwayne's mother. Put those paper plates and cups in the trash when you finish, she said. Did you draw that piano note back there? she asked Dwayne.

Larry Lime drew it.

Oh. It's good, she said to Larry Lime as she left.

When they finished eating, Larry Lime stood. Come in here a minute, he said to Dwayne as he headed for the storage room. Let me show you one more seventh thing.

Dwayne followed.

I'm learning these whole note scales that, like, in the key of C you can play C, D, and E, then these three black notes instead of just the B-flat. To move you on to F. It kind of lifts you from C to F when you're making that change. Thelonious Monk did that.

Who?

Thelonious Monk? The Bleeder knew him in New York. Piano player.

What's his real name?

Thelonious Monk. And listen to this. Larry Lime played.

The Bleeder showed you that?

Yeah, he plays guitar, but he plays piano too. He making me work hard. You have to be able sing notes you hear and then play notes you sing and memorize these chords. It's jazz. And there's this way you can kind of delay notes too—make a song swing.

What about that rooster? asked Dwayne. Me and Mickey Dean want to take him to *The Birds* at the Rialto. They been holding it over.

Anytime. I'll show you how to put him to sleep.

Dwayne thought about asking Larry Lime to go with them to the movie. But he couldn't do that. He couldn't hardly even think it.

Let's finish that sanding, said Larry Lime.

Yeah, before they get back.

I might come back later and practice some. I got to

learn these melodies with both hands. You want to go noodling in the morning?

Sure. Dwayne knew they'd be going to the Half Mile Pond and nobody would see them. They'd go to the colored part.

Have you been yet? asked Larry Lime.

Not yet.

We could leave from the end of the South Cut about seven o'clock. That's when I usually go. Bring some thick gloves and a bathing suit. You won't need nothing but your hands. I'll bring a tow sack, show you all about it.

Dwayne told his daddy he was going fishing at the Half Mile Pond. He didn't mention Larry Lime. The next morning, he drove the pickup with his rod and reel in back to the west end of the South Cut. Dusty had jumped into the truck bed. Dwayne saw Larry Lime waiting, throwing rocks into the trash dump. Larry Lime's dog, Scrap, was along. Dwayne stopped the truck, looked into the rearview mirror.

They started walking the half mile to the pond, a pond with a dock and a few rowboats for whites, and a dock for blacks toward the south end. A rough trail circled it, sometimes under high oaks, sometimes through thick brush. They each wore a bathing suit under their jeans. Dusty and Scrap followed. When the trail narrowed, Larry Lime led the way. They took a left at a fork and headed toward the dock used by blacks. Larry Lime wondered if Dwayne had ever gone to the Half Mile Pond that way. After about forty yards, they took another left. Scrap followed, quick-stepping. Dusty took longer strides.

Larry Lime learned noodling from Uncle Young, who learned from a man from Louisiana, a Cajun. Larry Lime once explained to Dwayne while they were refinishing a table: Find a hollow log, underwater, a nesting place. Springtime. A partner blocks off one end of the log if both ends are open, and you stick your hand in the open end, hoping a catfish is inside guarding the eggs. If you move your fist very slowly and the fish is big enough, he will swallow your hand, and you can grab a gill with your other hand and pull him out. You can also make a narrow wood box with the ends open, put it on the bottom in waist- or chest-deep water, and place a big rock on top of it. Something like that. Follow the same procedure.

If he ain't too big, said Larry Lime as they walked along, you can just catch his lower lip and squeeze and pull him out that way. If it's scaly, it's probably a carp. And if you feel a shell, it's a turtle. They're good to eat if it's the right kind. Mama can tell. I never studied no turtles. This Cajun knowed a guy that stuck his finger up in a beaver hole, 'cept he didn't know that, see, and he won't wearing gloves, and he felt this sting—*pow*—and pulled out his hand, and a finger stump was spurting blood. Larry Lime held up his index finger, bent, over his shoulder as they walked. 'Course gloves might not have made no difference, he said.

Damn. Your daddy don't noodle?

He went once, heard that story, then he said he'd been twice: first time and last time. But me and Uncle Young catched twenty-four catfish and a carp last summer, and the biggest catfish was thirteen pounds.

Damn.

Larry Lime stepped over a downed tree trunk.

Dwayne followed. What if it's a snake? he asked.

You move on to the next log.

Yeah. Huh. Walking behind Larry Lime, Dwayne looked at Larry Lime's hands as they walked. His palms were as white as Dwayne's.

They crossed another downed tree. The morning was hot already. The sun sparkled off high-up tree leaves.

Do you know the names of trees? asked Dwayne.

You mean like "Herman"?

Naw, man. Like oak, all that.

Not yet.

My daddy said he was walking through the woods with a couple of Yankees and one of them said, "What kind of tree is that?" and Daddy said, "That's one of our southern hardwoods."

Larry Lime didn't say anything. They walked for a while. Then he said, I don't get it.

You know, Daddy didn't know the names of the trees, so when he said "southern hardwoods" that shut up the Yankees, because they didn't know no better.

I ain't got nothing against no Yankee, said Larry Lime.

Yeah, some of them are okay. Daddy gets some at the shop.

They was pretty good back in the Civil War.

Has any of your people got bit? asked Dwayne.

Bit?

By a snake or something.

Me and Uncle Young ain't been bit. That's why you wear thick gloves. Them you got will be good.

Who else around here noodles?

Me and Uncle Young are the only colored noodlers I know.

They could now see the pond through the trees and brush. Larry Lime pulled back a low branch so they could move along the narrow path and down a high bank.

The guy that teached Uncle Young, said Larry Lime, he won't white. Well, maybe he was. A Cajun.

I never seen a Cajun, said Dwayne.

Here we are. Larry Lime found the short, flat board he'd left beside a tree. Take this, he said. That's all you need.

They pulled off their jeans and shirts and shoes, and in their bathing suits moved down the bank into knee-deep cool water. The bank behind them blocked the bright morning light. Out in the middle of the pond, where the sun shone, a mist lay along the surface. The dogs moved off into the woods.

We just go down along the edge here, said Larry Lime. Follow me. The bottom's pretty smooth. We can talk but it's got to be quiet. Up at the north end is where I got baptized. We're almost at the first gum.

Gum?

Larry Lime stopped, turned, showed with his hands. Like a rabbit box, he said, with the back end open. Big, long, hollow box. Like a hollow log. Uncle Young planted about six in here, made me promise not to show anybody, but I'll show you a couple. And I know where two hollow logs are.

As they waded along in waist-deep water, Larry Lime bent over, kneeled, moved slowly, his shoulders under the water. Okay, come around here now, he said, almost whispering. Right around there, and reach down and you'll feel the back end of what's like a rabbit box, and it's open and you got to close it off with that board, but you got to hold it tight up against the box with your hand or maybe your foot, and I'm going to come in from the front end. You might have to come around and back me up if I don't get a good hold on him.

Back you up?

Nevermind. Move in right there and see can't you find the back end of the box. Move slow, and talk quiet.

Dwayne was bending over, his chin touching the water. Okay, he said. Wait a minute. Okay, I got this end covered up. Man, this is spooky.

They were face to face, two heads three feet apart resting on brown water. Dwayne — for the first time — noticed a scar between Larry Lime's eyes.

Circles of small waves moved out from them, reached sunlight, where they sparkled and shimmered.

Here I go, said Larry Lime. His head went under. Came back up. Nothing in there, he said. Shit.

When Larry Lime was eleven, Uncle Young picked him up in the truck and brought him to a field beyond the north end of the pond. Ten or twelve cars were parked in the field. On the bank of the pond they sang

"Angel Band," and preacher Hobgood, the preacher back then, preached a sermon. Two women were baptized, one crying and waving her arms around, the other woman, blind and in ankle-deep water, was afraid to go deeper. Two of the women talked to her a long time. Deacon Morris came over and talked to her for a while. They calmed her into waist-deep water, where the preacher suddenly leaned her back and underwater, and Deacon Morris standing at her side held her elbow and helped her back to her feet. They started her out of the pond, and two women took over and led her out the rest of the way. Next were seven little girls dressed in white robes and white headscarves, and then Larry Lime and three other boys, two older, one younger. Larry Lime had gone down front in the church sanctuary to be saved because Aunt Marzie told him if he didn't he'd go to hell — and that in heaven they would eat at fine tables with everybody up there taking turns serving the food. Chances are, she said, that old man Fitzsimmons won't be in heaven, but if he is, he be putting that big plate of vegetables down right under your chin and pouring you the clearest, freshest water you ever tasted.

A short prayer was said over each child, the preacher holding his hand up toward heaven, elbow straight, as he prayed, the hand holding the handkerchief that was then placed over the child's mouth as he or she was pushed backward until the head was out of sight and then brought back up with all those attending saying Amen. Aunt Marzie saying what she usually said—My, my.

Dwayne, age twelve, had stood in the choir room above and behind the choir loft. A man and two women stood with him. He remembered wearing a white shirt buttoned to the neck. The preacher doing the baptizing was a stranger, the stranger who'd preached a week of revival meetings the week before, an old man, tall, who talked about his hands not being strong but his heart being full of God's love. He'd held up his hands so people could see his crooked fingers. The same man who'd talked about Jesus and heaven and the right hand of God talked with such persuasion that Dwayne had decided it would be a good idea to go ahead and join the church, to accept Jesus as his personal savior at the same age as his mama and daddy had. What could he possibly lose? And Mickey Dean and Donnie already had.

Larry Lime and Dwayne hand-fished a total of two boxes and two hollow logs. No luck. They dried off with their shirts, got dressed, and started home, the dogs behind them again.

The sun was getting up in the sky. As they walked,

Dwayne said, I keep thinking about that guy and the beaver.

Yeah. I think it was a hole in the bank or something. You ever heard of anybody losing a finger?

Daddy knew this guy when he was going to school got his finger stuck in a door, you know, in the crack next to the wall—in there, a big metal door, heavy thing—and it took it right off, and then there was all this scrambling around and nobody could find it. And then later on somebody found it in a chalk tray.

A chalk tray? said Larry Lime.

Yeah. And I got a buddy at school, his brother got his thumb pulled into the chain sprocket of a motor scooter and it took it right off.

They walked up to Dwayne's daddy's truck. Dwayne stopped at the tailgate and said, Daddy said he knew somebody lost his finger at a high-school football game when it got caught the wrong way between these two football helmets when they crashed together, and they stopped the game and everybody was looking for the finger on the field, and one of the coaches over at the sideline yelled out through a megaphone, "Check your cleats, boys."

Oh, damn, man. Larry Lime laughed. He cupped his mouth with his hand and in a deep voice said, Check your cleats, boys.

11

AN AUTO-REPAIR GARAGE was built onto the side of the Bone Brick Store. The store and repair shop and surrounding grounds were owned by Jesse Dillworth. He'd drive a car up on two wide, wall-like brick ramps, one under each wheel, ramps with a pit between them, and then he'd sit or kneel beneath the car to work on it. Near those ramps were the remains of another—a third low wall deserted when its twin was knocked down by a dump truck come to pick up old tires. This wall paralleled Prestonville Road. Boys sat there, sometimes as many as six or seven, guessing the year and make of passing automobiles. The angle of view allowed them to see the fronts of cars coming from north or south, from far enough away for suspense when someone called out a model and year. Because you had to make your guess only once, an early guess was often wrong.

From the brick wall you could hear the train whistle blowing at the North and South Cuts and at other crossings — and unless the wind was strong from the east, you could also hear the rumble, roar, and clanking.

All the boys on the wall were white, except when Larry Lime sat off to the side a little. His older brother, Tinker, sat there in the '50s. Tinker had since moved on to Detroit, and though he did come back once in a while, he didn't talk much and didn't go to church anymore.

When the talk shifted from cars to basketball, furniture refinishing, or popular music, Larry Lime sometimes had something to say. They all talked about high-school basketball teams or marching bands — Larry Lime played drums in the Sanding and Bonner High School marching band. Sanding and Bonner was down in Prestonville.

Out in front of the store, off to the side, was the work station where black men waited for work.

Beneath the roof that extended over the front of the store and the two gas pumps, men stood and talked, mostly white men, though on occasion a black man joined them.

Larry Lime walked around and sat in his spot on the end of the wall. The school bus had just let him off. It was Thursday after school.

Hey, mens, he said.

Dwayne, Donnie, Ray Wheeler, Mickey Dean, and Mickey Dean's little brother, Vince, sat on the wall. They all, except for Larry Lime, wore dark socks and Bass Weejun shoes. Mickey Dean had learned about dark socks in *Esquire* magazine and introduced them to the boys. White socks were the style before that. Larry Lime wore the overalls he wore most days, and the high-top Converse All Stars that once belonged to Donnie. Aunt Marzie, who worked at Donnie's and Dwayne's houses, had brought them home and given them to him.

Dwayne's transistor radio lay beside his leg on the wall. The radio, about the size of a hymn book, fit inside a tight leather case that had holes over the speaker. It used D batteries and was tuned to WSSB. "Big Boss Man" was playing.

I can play that, said Mickey Dean. It's easy. That shuffle thing in E. Kind of like in "Flip, Flop, and Fly." *Ba-do ba-do ba-do ba-do*. Fifty-six Chevy.

Check, said Donnie. I'm still ahead by two.

That's one now, said Dwayne.

That part, said Larry Lime, soun' like "Mean Old World" speeded up. And some other Little Walter songs. He got a bunch of songs like that. Jimmy Reed, he just stay in one place on the harp, and Little Walter, he move around. Larry Lime brought his hands to his mouth like he was playing a harmonica.

Fifty-nine Mercury, said Donnie.

Sixty, said Dwayne.

Wrong, fifty-nine. Mickey Dean?

Fifty-nine.

Aw shit, man.

My mama got the .45, said Larry Lime. "Mean Old World."

Up three. Me.

Larry Lime's got a Blue Horse notebook with music stuff in it, Dwayne started to say, but didn't say. Drawings, notes, he didn't say.

Mickey Dean said, Jimmy Reed's wife has got to stand behind him at concerts and hold him up 'cause he gets so drunk. And tell him the words to songs.

She sing harmony with him too, said Larry Lime.

We could do "Big Boss Man," said Dwayne. He wondered, Who's going to play the harp? He wondered if Larry Lime could play harp. Who is Little Walter? he asked Larry Lime.

Is he any kin to Little Richard? asked Donnie.

Little Bo Peep, said Mickey Dean. Little Weenie McGhee.

He's this singer play the harp, said Larry Lime. Naw, he ain't no kin to Little Richard. How's y'all's band doing?

It's coming pretty good, said Dwayne.

We got the Dell brothers, said Donnie. Trumpet and sax. They do some rhythm and blues, man.

Sixty-two Chevy, said Donnie. Impala.

That's right.

Extra credit.

We ain't playing that way, said Dwayne.

Mickey Dean said to Larry Lime, Dwayne said we could use your chicken for the TV audition. I want to see that, man.

Oh, yeah. Larry Lime smiled, wiped his nose. Her name's Redbird. Just put down a flat, round pan and she jumps on it and starts dancing—he paused—no joke.

They talked about piano players for a while. Ray Wheeler had said he was learning three Fats Domino songs. Dwayne tried to think about Larry Lime as the band's piano player. What if Ray quit for some reason? Could they ask Larry to join them? No.

Mickey Dean spoke up. Daddy said we could write "The Amazing Rumblers" on the side of the hearse, if we can do it with some kind of removable tape.

Larry Lime pictured a black hearse with white tape on the side.

The brick wall was feeling hard to Dwayne. He pushed himself up, let himself back down.

The talk went to basketball, marbles — a taw that three boys won championships with — school bus driving, Shirley Bushnell's letting Mike Granger and Fess Clingstead finger her at the Moss Level Swimming Pool. Dwayne wondered if it were true. Shirley had given him a note in English class, asking him to help her with an Algebra assignment.

Mickey Dean slid down off the wall, asked Dwayne so the others couldn't hear, We going to drop that rooster out of the balcony tomorrow night?

Yeah, said Dwayne. He slid down from the wall, stepped over to Larry Lime. How about if we drive by your house, he said, and get the rooster tomorrow night, and you show me how to put him to sleep. We ain't got to turn him loose until eight fourteen. That's the first good scene. I timed it out.

I'll meet you at the end of South Cut anytime after six.

Make it seven.

Okay.

12

At eight o'clock Friday night, Dwayne and Mickey Dean walked along Sixth Street in Whittier. Dwayne wore a hunting coat. The rooster was under the coat—but not asleep.

That ticket lady gone think it's strange, said Mickey Dean, you wearing that coat.

It's hot too. Let's step in here. They stepped into an alley. The chicken clucked. As Dwayne pulled him out, a wing got away, flapped wildly.

Hold both wings! said Mickey Dean.

I know. Dwayne got control, held both wings down. Help me get his head under this wing. Dwayne lifted a wing, pulled it forward. Mickey Dean tucked in the rooster's head, Dwayne covered it with the wing and held on tight. He lowered the rooster to just above his ankles and with straight arms began to slowly swing him like a clock pendulum, but higher and more briskly. Three, four, five, six, he counted out loud. At twenty he stopped. The chicken was still. He placed the chicken back under his coat, pressing it against his chest. Let's go, he said.

Back on the sidewalk, they walked up to the movie-theater ticket window. Dwayne stood back and Mickey Dean paid. The same old lady as always. Dwayne managed to look at his watch. Four minutes until release time.

They walked up the stairs to the balcony, Dwayne in front. At the top of the stairs in a lobby area, the chicken started fluttering, one wing loose under Dwayne's coat. No one was in sight, and through the door to the balcony came the sounds of two women talking on-screen.

Get the head back under the wing, said Mickey Dean.

That's what I'm trying to do.

At least he ain't hollering.

Dwayne reach inside the coat. I got the head, he said. It's back under his wing. I got him. Now...how can I swing him?

I don't know, said Mickey Dean. Take him out of

the damn coat. No, wait. Take off your coat and wrap that around him. Have you got a good hold?

Yeah, but how can I take my coat off and hold the chicken at the same time? What time is it?

Mickey Dean looked at his watch. About a minute and a half, I think.

Help me.

The rooster was moving its legs as if running slowly.

Okay, said Dwayne. Look. You hold the chicken under the—

Is the head still under the wing?

Yes!

Just hand me the damn chicken and take your coat off, said Mickey Dean.

You reach *in* and get him.

They both looked around to be sure nobody was watching.

Mickey Dean reached under Dwayne's jacket and pulled out the rooster, head beneath a wing. Dwayne quickly removed his coat, wrapped it around the chicken. On the movie screen, hundreds of crows perched restlessly side by side along telephone wires and on monkey bars next to a schoolhouse.

Mickey Dean looked at his watch. We can make it, he said. Hurry up. Swing him.

Dwayne started swinging the large bundle back and forth.

On-screen, two women and some children were starting down the steps of the schoolhouse.

A nervous mother seated in the balcony, eyes on the crows, grabbed her small son's arm and said, We gettin' out of here. Coming through the balcony door she saw two white boys, one bending over slightly, swinging a bundle back and forth and counting.

The little boy stopped. The mother kept going, pulling his arm. She stopped.

The boy said, What you-all doing?

Dwayne said, Nothing.

Be quiet, the mother said to the boy. Come on.

We're putting a chicken to sleep, said Mickey Dean. He looked at Dwayne.

You come on here, the mother said to the child, pulling him toward the stairs.

They putting a chicken to sleep, said the little boy.

Hush up.

Twenty, said Dwayne. They both started through the balcony door, Dwayne in the lead holding the bundle tight. A dozen or so people sat along the front balcony rail in the middle section. On the big screen, screaming children ran down a hill, crows flapped along just above their heads, latching onto children's hair, pecking for eyes, drawing blood. Dwayne, with Mickey Dean following, entered the front row to his right, where no one was sitting.

The auditorium below was two-thirds full.

The chicken felt big and warm under the coat.

Now, Mickey Dean whispered. Now!

Dwayne maneuvered an arm inside the coat, pulled out the chicken as his coat fell to the floor, shook the rooster to awaken him, and pushed/threw him out above the audience. Dwayne's heart was pumping, ready for the blossom into full flight, the fluttering, the cackling, the landing on people, the screaming.

The chicken, like a partially inflated basketball, landed in the far aisle, bounced, lay still.

What the hell? said Dwayne. He looked at Mickey Dean. Crow caws and children's screams sounded throughout the theater. Reflections from the screen played on Mickey Dean's face.

I killed the damn thing, said Dwayne.

What?

I killed it.

You didn't *kill* it. Did you?

That's a dead chicken. But I think that's going to be all right with Larry Lime. I think we smothered him or something.

Dwayne watched a man sitting next to the chicken look down at the big lump of feathers. The man reached forward, tapped the woman in front of him. She turned. He pointed to the still rooster.

The action on the screen was quieting.

You think he might be still asleep? whispered Mickey Dean.

The chicken is dead.

The woman screamed. People turned. Another woman looked at the chicken and screamed. The man pushed the chicken away with his foot as if it smelled bad, looked toward the back of the theater and then up toward the balcony.

Dwayne sat quickly, pulled Mickey Dean down by the arm.

Let's go get him, said Mickey Dean. See if he wakes up. Then wait till the next big scene. Make this thing work.

No, said Dwayne. It's over. The chicken's dead. He's got to be.

Somebody in the middle section of the balcony called out, Was that a chicken?

Mickey Dean looked over. Naw, he said. He threw my coat.

That was a *chicken,* what you say.

Let's go, said Dwayne.

In the downstairs lobby Dwayne said, I'll go get him.

Dwayne, wearing his hunting coat, walked toward the rooster. Things were calm on the screen. He reached for the rooster's feet. The man looked at him and the woman turned.

Somebody dropped this chicken from the balcony, Dwayne whispered. We caught them.

The chicken felt heavy, and as Dwayne lifted him by his feet, the wings dropped open limply. Then he lifted it higher, folded in the wings, and as he walked up the aisle he managed to slip it into the game pouch in the back of his coat.

He met Mickey Dean outside on the sidewalk.

Where is he?

He got away.

I told you. I told you he won't dead.

13

In the middle of the rear wall inside Liberty Day of Reckoning A.M.E. Church sanctuary, just above head height, was a window. The window looked out from a small room with a five-and-a-half-foot ceiling and over the back of the heads of everybody for a view of the preacher and the choir behind him.

Mr. Stalls, who spent a good bit of time in that room, wore wire-rimmed glasses, and his hair was mostly gray. He had electrical cords running all over the church and out to the nursery, so that nursery workers could hear the sermon.

Reverend Manning had replaced Reverend Clement Dill as pastor in 1960. Mr. Dill, after a severe heart attack, called on Reverend Manning to come in as interim preacher. Dr. Manning liked the church—especially its potential, with folks coming south from Whittier and north from West Preston. He liked it so much he sent for his family and stayed on.

Manning was from northern Virginia. He insisted that the choir wear robes, and three families left the church because of the robes. Mrs. Manning had children's group piano lessons with wooden keyboards on Wednesday nights. Mr. Stalls made the keyboards.

After seeing Mr. Stalls's intercom setup, Reverend Manning bought a portable tape recorder, one of the small new portables—reel-to-reel. He preached into a microphone on the podium, and the music and message were recorded on the recorder set up in the little room in back. Mr. Stalls monitored the recorder during the service. Wires all around. Mr. Stalls and Dr. Manning shared a dream that a cardboard box with a few reels of sermons would eventually grow into a library that could be shipped all over the world. In the meantime, the recordings went out to shut-ins as far away as Whittier and West Preston.

Within a month or two, the white church, Starke Baptist, got word of the idea and started their own recording distribution to shut-ins.

Larry Lime was one of the first to carry tapes to the shut-ins. When he realized he could use the recorder to tape his Friday lessons with the Bleeder on the back side of the sermon tape, he volunteered to do all of the tape deliveries. Uncle Young let him use his trash truck—the one with plywood sides, not the refrigerated meat-run truck belonging to Mr. Fitzsimmons.

Mr. and Mrs. Bissett were shut-ins. At their house in West Starke, Mrs. Bissett would come each Sunday afternoon to the front door and invite Larry Lime on back to a little sitting room with their cuspidors and a stack of magazines and an Emerson cabinet TV. Larry Lime would place the recorder so they could hear the service. Mr. Bissett would always be sitting back there waiting when Larry Lime and Mrs. Bissett entered the room, and Larry Lime would sit for a minute before leaving.

Mrs. Bissett, a small woman, talked ninety miles an hour, and Mr. Bissett, he'd just sit and listen to her.

One day while they all sat, the sun—through open window blinds—shined into Larry Lime's eyes, and Mrs. Bissett said to Mr. Bissett, Sweetheart, shut them blinds so the sun won't be in that boy's eyes.

Mr. Bissett stood, shuffled over to the blinds, and pulled the cord, shutting them. He was a hundred years old; she was ninety-nine. They'd been married seventy-five years, and people were wondering how much longer he was going to keep on driving his '39 Ford. Everybody talked about it, talked about how much those two had seen, born during the Civil War, how they both had missed only a few Sundays in church, the same church after all those years, spending hours every Sunday inside four walls where they experienced a God they knew nowhere else, a God who got them out of bed day after day.

On the first meat run after his visit, Larry Lime told Uncle Young that Mrs. Bissett had said, "Sweetheart, shut them blinds so the sun won't be in that boy's eyes." She been calling him sweetheart seventy-five years, Larry Lime said.

Uncle Young looked at Larry Lime for a few seconds from over behind the steering wheel, placed the tip of his Pall Mall against the vent window, and said, You know *why* she still calling him sweetheart, Knothead?

Nossuh.

Because she can't remember his name.

14

Man, said Larry Lime, that Pat Boone "Tutti Frutti," that's *lame*, man.

The boys sat on the wall, talking about Little Richard.

Can you say that *whop bop* part? Dwayne asked Larry Lime.

A-whop bop-a-lu-ma ba-lop bam bam. Something like that.

Mickey Dean said, It's *bop bop ah-lew-bop a-bop bam boom.*

That's pretty close, said Larry Lime.

I learned it, man.

A wall of dark clouds was rising in the west, and the sun was sinking behind the upper rim of the clouds, bringing a sobering shadow over the store. A cool breeze was working up.

Fifty-two Chevy.

Fifty-one. Fifty-five Ford. I got 'em both. That's a fifty-one Chevy, man.

They watched black cars from the forties go by, some from the thirties, cars of bright Hawaiian colors from the fifties — the mustard yellow and white of the fifty-five Ford owned by Dwayne's uncle Don and aunt Pam.

Each boy had an idea of his ideal car. Larry Lime loved the look of Flash's '39 Ford coupe, the choppiness of it. Its rear end had a silent meanness and good manners about it — a facial expression. Larry Lime rode in it when they picked up chairs or small tables. The inside smelled like cigarettes. Up on the dashboard was a bottle of Listerine, half full or so, one or two open packs of Chesterfields, furniture refinishing orders, receipts, other stuff. Flash rarely spoke to Larry Lime directly, except to tell him what to do. He kept the white sidewall tires on that car whitened and blackened with canned paste.

Flash would be taking a break on the lawn, over near his Ford, outside the range of the paint remover. Larry Lime, brushing Remove-All onto a dresser or chair, would glance at Flash, checking to see when he was about to start back in. Flash usually squatted, sat on his heels almost, smoked a cigarette, the short butt between his thumb and index and middle fingers, the ash glow toward his palm, the wet end to his lips, and he'd finish smoking it, lick his fingers and thumb, and pinch out the fire, field-strip it, ball up the paper into a tiny ball, drop it, stand and brush his pants down the front, and walk back to the shop to give instructions, do some work himself.

Dwayne thought again about maybe asking Shirley Bushnell for a date. Dwayne imagined being with Shirley in his daddy's Buick. Linda would be upset, but she wouldn't do anything. She wouldn't break up with him.

Flash walked around the corner and toward the wall. Dwayne thought he had a walk kind of like Paul Newman in that movie *Hud*, and there seemed to be some Warren Oates in him too — the look.

Larry Lime worried his thumb cuticle with the nail of his index finger.

You two gone be late for work, Flash said to Dwayne and Larry Lime, pointing toward them with fingers holding an unlit cigarette. We got them two dressers to do. He clicked open his flip-top lighter, lit his cigarette, clapped it shut.

When you going to audition for Bobby Reese? Dwayne asked him.

Soon as I can.

We are too.

Who? Flash looked at Larry Lime.

Our band. We're going to learn a couple of country songs.

Good luck. When?

In a few weeks. We just got to work up two songs.

They'll only pick one act, so don't audition when I do if you want to get on the show. Flash started back to the front of the store. You guys better not be late, he said over his shoulder.

We can be five minutes late, said Dwayne. You ain't there yet.

Flash stopped, turned. The foreman ain't ever late, he said. He looked at Larry Lime, then back to Dwayne. I didn't know Jesse allowed niggers on the wall.

Yes, you did, Dwayne started to say.

15

LARRY LIME HAD LEARNED "The Preacher," "Summertime," "Take the 'A' Train," "St. Louis Blues," and "Blue Monk," and he'd repaired three notes inside the storage room piano so that everything was playing just right except for the bottom three keys, the ones he'd pirated.

On this summer Thursday, while they worked in the shop, Larry Lime and Dwayne talked about music:

Live at the Apollo is *something*, man, Larry Lime said. It's got "Night Train," but different than the old jazz versions. Way different. This one got the strong beat on the *one*, man. Larry Lime stood from where he was sitting — sanding the front of a drawer — lifted his foot, and brought it down on that one beat, on the

DAT as he sang the instrumental part: *DAT da-da da-da da-da DAT da-da da-da da-da. DA-DA. BAM. BAM. BAM.* Foot down again on the one beat, dropping his head to the side on the one beat. This "Night Train's" better, man. A whole different thing. And he's got a little bit of "Please, Please, Please" on there. That's the one he fall down on and all that. You-all ought to do all of that one. You ought to sing it, do some of his steps, man. I can show you some, and I can record the album on a reel-to-reel tape and bring this tape recorder I got. Keep it over here some. Want me to bring it?

Yeah. Sure.

You and your band can learn the whole album and stop and start the sound on the tape and back it up to the right place like I'm doing. Some radio stations playing the whole album like it was just one song. "I feel awwwwwright. You know, I feel awright, chil'ren. I feel awwwwaaawwwwwawwright." Sing it.

Dwayne tried. "I feel awwwwright. You know, I feel awright, chil'ren."

That's pretty good.

Larry thought about trying to explain his favorite song, "Blue Monk," to Dwayne. But he needed to back off some. He knew better than to go down into what all he was finding in jazz music. All that was too much.

He felt a magic in "Blue Monk" that he'd not known before with any church songs, or blues, or from anywhere else, though it did have a kind of muscle in it like a gospel song. It moved to places he expected it to move, but then it *didn't*. He felt the strange rhythm shift at the end of the first time through...and he knew it *belonged*. The ending phrase had popped up, come in early, but then the song waited, made up for the rush. He wanted to play it, wanted to understand that rhythm shift, to make that a part of what he knew, could play. He felt that Mr. Monk had written it for him. The Bleeder said Monk was from North Carolina, that Mary Lou Williams was big on him from way, way back. She was a jazz woman. He'd seen a picture of the Monk in a hat without a brim. The Bleeder talked about how Monk stood up and danced, or left the bandstand for a drum solo or a saxophone solo. Up in New York City. Larry Lime had saved his furniture money and bought a Monk album, listened to all of the songs, and studied some. Those songs were different somehow than the others the Bleeder was giving him to record onto his reel-to-reel tape, the ones he was learning. The Monk songs had places in them that were crooked or "off" — strange notes and rhythms popped up here and there. They seemed like they were part of the future.

There were some sort of crooked places in James Brown's songs too. WSSB was now playing *Live at the Apollo* almost every day. Larry Lime was picking out chords from the songs, studying the rhythms.

By moving an old red Naugahyde couch and a couple of other things in the furniture-storage room, the Amazing Rumblers had space to stand as if they were on a stage. They practiced on Saturday afternoons and one night during the week.

Their first real-live gig—at the Youth Center in Whittier—was on a Friday in June. Several parents had formed a club for teenagers who were too young to drive. They all gathered at the Ruritan building on Saturday nights from six thirty till ten and danced to .45 records: "April Love," "Smoke Gets in Your Eyes," "Long Tall Sally." Parent chaperones provided punch and cookies on a long table. At one end of the dance floor was a Ping-Pong table for the boys. The Amazing Rumblers were the Youth Club's first live act.

Dwayne's daddy had constructed for Willy, the bass player, a speaker cabinet that held two twelve-inch speakers. He'd also made a cabinet for the glow-tubed innards of a jukebox that served as a speaker amp for Ray. Mickey Dean had a store-bought amp for his guitar.

*   *   *

One night soon after the Youth Center gig, Dwayne laid the reel-to-reel tape-recorder microphone in front of his phonograph speaker, dropped the arm and needle onto the LP album *Live at the Apollo*, and pressed record and forward on the recorder. The phonograph and tape recorder both rested on a small table, the recorder with two reels sitting like dessert plates on the machine—a small machine, not one of the larger uprights. The tape, extending between the reels, ran through a narrow slot. Five buttons just below the slot were labeled play, reverse, rewind, fast forward, and record. Dwayne walked over, sat on the couch, closed his eyes, and listened, trying to see the band performing. He was singing. He was James Brown. The idea, the vision came: The Amazing Rumblers memorizing the songs and spoken words on the LP, getting everything *exactly* like it was on the record. Exactly. No breaks between songs. Constant music for over a half hour. And he'd dance like James Brown. It would be electric. It would be an explosion.

They wouldn't get on Bobby Reese's show with *that* music, but they'd get on something, somewhere.

At the next practice, Dwayne announced his vision. The band would have to start learning the whole *Live at the Apollo* album. Word for word. Note for note. He played the reel-to-reel tape of the entire album for the band.

There was no hesitation from any band member. They would learn it.

Outside, in front of the shop, Larry Lime and Flash were completing a Fitzsimmons refinishing job.

Who wants to be the announcer there at the start? said Dwayne.

I'll be the announcer, said Gaston.

The boys were stationed in a U shape facing the refinishing-room door. They'd moved a table and the couch out of the way.

He's got the voice, said Darren, Gaston's brother.

Okay, Gaston, said Dwayne, I got it written down right here. "Ladies and gentlemen, it's star time. Are you ready for star time?"

Should I say it like a nigger?

Yeah, but don't say that.

What?

Nigger.

Why?

Because. Go ahead.

Ladies and gentlemen, said Gaston, it's star time —

Wait a minute, said Dwayne. Listen to this so you'll get the idea.

Dwayne turned on the machine. *Ladies and Gentlemen, it's star time. Are you ready for star time? Okay, say it.*

Ladies and Gentlemen, it's star time. Are you ready for star time?

Try it with the whole *tone* thing in there so that you're saying it with some gumption, said Dwayne. He rewound the tape, played the short speech. This is great music, man, he said. He looked from one set of eyes to the next, gauged who believed him. We got to get it all just right, he said, just exactly like it is on the album. Thirty-five minutes or so. And then that can be a part of every show we do. Go ahead, Gaston.

Gaston recited the intro.

Dwayne said, You're saying "nationally and internationally known." It's "national and international known." See. It's written down there. You got to get it right. And say *hardest* working man in show business. Come down on *hardest.*

Why don't *you* do it? said Gaston.

Because I'm James Brown, man.

PART II

16

FLASH'S MAMA and Donnie's mama, Mrs. Howell, visited each other once or twice a month for
conversation.

Donnie's Mama talked about Donnie's loud drum
set. It was like some kind of, I don't know, car wreck
that just kept going on and on in there in his room
until he finally carted them across the street to the
furniture shop. And now that music they're doing over
there is like a *train* wreck.

Donnie's Mama could speak with her sad eyes,
with her downcast nature, the whole language of her
body saying—mostly in her own home with her family: You better watch out now because I'm kind of wilt-
ing because of what you just said or did or are about to

say, and if I wilt there's going to be a collapse of the system, which is this house and food and care and my kind of love, which is big hugs and proclamations of love and concern, and besides all that, I'm the only one Aunt Marzie will listen to. You all know that.

Some evenings, Aunt Marzie took home half a ham or half a pie or half a chicken, two dollars maybe—or some change, a pair of shoes, a jug of apple cider. It was about the same at Dwayne's Mama's, where Aunt Marzie also worked, except she was paid more and didn't have to return the jug.

Donnie's Mama asked Flash's Mama, Do you think it's okay they play them rock and roll songs? I told Donnie it was enough him playing in the school band without doing that rock and roll.

I don't think it does any harm, said Flash's Mama, as long as it's not that bong-bong race music. It's everywhere now. I'm glad Flash ain't got into it—that I know of. He loves that little guitar his daddy left him, and it sounds real good—it's not electrified you know. I reckon it's *electric* music they're playing over there, right?

Oh, yes, said Donnie's Mama. I can sit on the porch and hear it—the rumble from it. Drowns out the dern train. Well, it don't drawn out the *train*, but you know.... 'Course Swansee don't seem to mind.

Well, said Flash's Mama—and she raised both eyebrows just a little—Swansee don't seem to mind a whole lot. Her and Marcus got all that income from everybody in Whittier and Starke and Prestonville getting their furniture refinished at Marcus's shop. And Jared Fitzsimmons with all his antiques giving them all his business. But I don't think I'd want colored people working in my backyard.

Except it's been done for centuries, said Donnie's Mama. It's a good thing our forefathers didn't feel like you, else there wouldn't have been any plantations.

I don't think my people missed out on much. Them plantations were set up to keep rich people from working. I read about that one time. What they wanted was a leisure class that could paint pictures and read books. I remember reading that and thinking, *What would you learn in a leisure class?* And then I learned a few years later about the middle class, lower class, upper class. The leisure class was gone with the Civil War. Gone with the wind. Did you ever study about that? asked Flash's Mama.

No, said Donnie's Mama. Not that I recall. Except I can say I don't know what we'd do without Aunt Marzie.

I just hope I don't ever need any kind of help around the house. 'Course I don't keep the cleanest house in the world either. And I ain't got a husband and young children and all, which makes it lots easier on me.

That night at Donnie's, Donnie's daddy said, Pass me some more of them butterbeans.

Donnie's mother passed him the butterbeans, and he spooned the last of them and said, Aunt Marzie, can you bring us some more butterbeans in here?

Aunt Marzie was eating in the kitchen. *Man'll be farting all night,* she thought. The family was eating a bit early because they were all going to a Saturday night movie, *Bye Bye Birdie,* with some actors and actresses Aunt Marzie couldn't remember the names of.

She walked into the dining room with the pot of butterbeans, filled the bowl on the table. She'd take home the remainder of the butterbeans, and what was left of the squash and the chicken and dumplings.

Every weekday when Donnie's daddy, the deputy sheriff, drove Aunt Marzie home—he didn't want her to walk—and turned in Aunt Marzie's driveway off Luther's Chin Road beside Larry Lime's house, nobody took second notice because this driving her home business had been going on for nineteen years. Sometimes Larry Lime was in the yard or at the chicken pen and saw them pass by. He wondered how the siren and the red blinking light on top of the car were turned on and off. A switch? A button you pressed?

Don't you want some more butterbeans? said Donnie's mother to Crystal, Donnie's seven-year-old sister.

Now the child be farting all night, thought Aunt Marzie. *She done ate her plate clean.*

I o-'ont no more, said Crystal.

Thank God, thought Aunt Marzie.

Donnie said, I'll take some more.

Donnie was beating on his thigh with his fork and spoon, trying out that new marching drumbeat that Mr. Allen had brought in from somewhere, with syncopated beats coming in the last two measures, rushing that last beat a little bit to get that syncopated kick. Mr. Allen heard it just last year when the Sanding and Bonner High band, Larry Lime's band, marched for the first time ever in the Whittier Christmas parade.

17

Dwayne followed Larry Lime from outside through the back door of the shop and into the practice room. Larry Lime had Redbird in a tow sack and was carrying a big, round tin pan. Dwayne closed the back door. I don't want Dusty in here, he said.

Larry Lime let Redbird out of the sack, dropped the pan onto the floor. The chicken stepped onto it and started scratching—or dancing.

Sort of pat your foot and she'll keep at it, said Larry Lime. He pulled a few corn-bread crumbs from his pocket and tossed them on the pan. Redbird pecked and kept dancing.

Dwayne stepped over and pushed the stop button on the recorder. "Night Train" from *Live at the Apollo* was playing. He turned it up. Redbird kept dancing. I wonder, said Dwayne, if the band playing will scare her.

You'll have to try it, said Larry Lime. He picked up Redbird, placed her back in the tow sack. See, that's all you do, he said. Now let me show you them dance steps. All you do is put this foot around behind this one like this, and then you turn, like this, but once you get back here you just keep turning like this till you back where you started from.

Dwayne moved a stand-up mirror from the other room. Flash was out on a delivery. The gin fan was going. Back in the storage room, Dwayne set up the mirror, practiced the maneuver while looking at himself.

Okay, that's good, said Larry Lime. He turned the recorder off. And then, he said, it's just this little shuffle you can do anyway you want to, but you do the shuffle, see, like this. You got to do it real fast. Something like this…

Dwayne tried it.

No, he said, like this. And you're keeping time with the music. You just come right back with this foot and you got to kind of twist like this, up on your toes but not all the way on your toes…That's good. That's pretty good. But faster…Go ahead…Yeah, that's it. And you can do it any way you want to, except you got to kinda move sometimes so it seem like you ain't moving at all, but your feet is.

Larry Lime rewound the tape.

They practiced for a while.

Okay, said Larry Lime. Let me run this ahead to "Please, Please, Please" ... Okay, there. To fall down, you just fall down, but be sure it's on both knees, straight down after you got this little squat going, and you gone almost kiss the microphone like it's a lady in a movie. Here ... but no, look, when you start down, pick up the back end of it so it's almost like you holding a guitar. That's good.

Flash walked in from the main room. What the hell, man? he said.

Dwayne stood looking at him. We're just ... we're just working on something for the band.

You-all *dancing* together?

He's showing me some stuff for the band. Naw, we ain't dancing together.

Goddamn, man, said Flash, and he turned, walked back into the refinishing room. Man, oh man, he said.

He don't mean no harm, said Dwayne.

I think I know what he mean. What his mama mean.

You know her? asked Dwayne.

She say some bad stuff to Aunt Marzie.

When?

A while back, out at the store.

She looks kind of like a mole, said Dwayne.

She some kin to you, ain't she?

Dwayne looked at Larry Lime. Well, yeah, she's my daddy's cousin.

She act like a mole too, said Larry Lime, watching Dwayne carefully. What I hear about her.

She talks a lot, said Dwayne.

Back when they was doing the sit-ins, Flash told Tinker he was going to Greensboro and kill one of them sit-in guys. You remember — at the lunch counters?

Yeah, but he didn't mean that. And they were kind of overdoing it, don't you think? Those guys.

Larry Lime wasn't sure what Dwayne meant. The lunch counter guys? he said. He looked at Dwayne — Dwayne's blond hair down over an eye. I would have went up there if I'd been older, he said. Tinker went but they didn't have nothing for him to do, and he says lots more stuff like that coming. They might do one up at Ed's Diner. That's what I heard.

A sit-in?

Oh, yeah.

18

LARRY LIME SAT onstage at the Frog behind the
yellow electric piano, the Bleeder just across from him.
The Bleeder's red guitar was strapped across his shoul-
ders. They'd just finished going through the chords to
"Sweet Georgia Brown" in the keys of F, B-flat, and
E-flat.

This whole business of "soul" music, said The
Bleeder. The Supremes and all that "A Hundred Pounds
of Clay"—stuff like that. What's his name, McDan-
iels? It's pitiful. Got white creeping in all over. Fluff.
Soft-edge crap. That's why you learning jazz.

The Bleeder explained that what he was teaching
Larry Lime had math in it, and patterns and blues and
slanky sounds, but it was solid in some way and moved

on more planes than a flat one. It moved in a cube. It was not soft stuff. You had to work to get it, and when you got it, it lasted. It was fun. It was like you'd played with somebody better than you—something that always happened—and you learned something, came out on the other side stronger. And then it got even more fun.

The Bleeder told Larry Lime that he cried the first time he heard Monk's song "Misterioso." A piano player named Robin Taylor was playing it slow, and the Bleeder said he cried because of one note that moved unexpectedly. He'd played it for Larry Lime, and now Larry Lime was learning it.

The Bleeder nodded for Larry Lime to commence his own arrangement of "Blue Monk." Larry Lime had decided he liked it a little slower than the recording. He began playing. He felt like it was his own song, that it had been with him always. As Larry Lime played, the Bleeder picked up his guitar.

Uncle Young stepped in at the door, sat on the bouncer's stool, listened, then left to take the afternoon's trash to the dump.

Larry Lime walked home by the tracks. When in range, he looked toward the shop. He was thinking about playing "Blue Monk" for Dwayne.

After leaving the tracks, he sat on a rock by the

lowland, looking down into that long hall-like section of woods. Sometimes the crows were out there in front of him. Over a period of months, he'd thrown corn bread from his pocket closer and closer to where he was sitting. Coal, the one he'd named, came nearest.

He pictured his arm long enough to reach deep into the woods, along that bottom, his hand finding God, out of sight, sitting back in there somewhere with Monk, maybe. At church, God was all mixed in with people noise and music noise. Maybe God rested in the lowland there in front of him.

God was supposed to deliver his people, but it seemed to Larry Lime that he did it only in church, unless Martin Luther King and his people were doing something. In church there was plenty of talk of God and Jesus and Moses and the promised land and David. Tinker told him that up north, they talked about a preacher who'd heard directions from God because of what he was reading about Moses and the promised land and slavery and the Egyptians, and he'd had things backfire on him.

Reverend Manning talked about Martin Luther King sometimes, and he talked about some other people. He said the Devil was all in among colored and white, but it seemed to Larry Lime that the Devil might be afraid of some white people.

If he walked along that low-lying stretch out in front of him—the lowland, that hallway—he would have come to the site of the old plantation. Only by excavating would he have found traces of it, the base of a slave-built foundation covered by pine straw and mulch. His great-uncles and aunts and cousins had walked the road in front of him not that long ago, bringing cotton and tobacco and white clay to the small loading station at the railroad track. He knew some of their names.

Aunt Marzie had told some of the stories while standing at that freestanding sink in her kitchen. A pipe stuck up through the floor and then turned at right angles so that the faucet ended up pointing down into the sink—but the pipe came in at the side of the sink, not the back.

Kids stood around her. It's the love of money, honey, she'd say. It's in the Bible. That's what caused them white mens to go off looking for slaves. It's whatever it is that's connected to the love of money. If they had the grace God give them to work for theirselves rather than having somebody else do it, then they wouldn't needed to buy slaves. And sometimes you got to have money, but you don't never need a lot of it. And if you do, you better watch out 'cause you'll get to loving it. Then the Devil'll get you.

The grandchildren had all heard the money talk and other lectures, but they didn't mind because it meant a story was coming. "The Goose and the Golden Egg," "The Starchy Shirt," "The Pig that Ate the Wolf," "The Worm and the Centipede."

You all sit down on that couch and Aunt Marzie'll tell you a story, she'd say. She'd clear her throat, a sound that reminded Aunt Marzie of her mother clearing *her* throat.

The crows cawed loudly, frantically, on the next Sunday after worship service at Liberty Day Church, most flying back and forth between two big trees not far down in the woods—trees taller than those around them. The crows glided from one tree to the other with their big feet hanging. Larry Lime wanted to understand what they were cawing about. He thought about *The Birds*, the rooster, what Dwayne had told him about it. How the rooster had sailed through the air, dead.

He walked into the edge of the woods, expecting to see an owl or a hawk sitting in a tree, the crows after it, but he couldn't see why they were uneasy. A crow cawed in midair, sort of bounced in a kind of midflight hiccup.

Larry Lime walked a little farther into the woods.

Crows flew from a pecan tree—or was it hickory?—
with nuts in their mouths. Other crows were flying
overhead, coming in from far away it looked like. He
heard his mother calling. No, that wouldn't be a pecan
tree. He turned and looked in his mother's direction.
She was at the edge of the parking lot. Larry Lime
glanced up at the railroad track. A man and woman sat
up there, looking at him.

19

WHEN FLASH WALKED in the back door of his mama's house, back from fishing at Half Mile Pond with a couple of his buddies from Prestonville, he noticed his mama's little stepladder on its side in the kitchen. He called out, Mama?

No answer.

Mama?

He started down the short hall. He heard a moan. He walked into her bedroom. She lay on her back on the floor, wearing her dark brown blouse and white and brown flowery pants, her left leg angled out from a spot between the knee and hip at a sickening forty-five-degree angle—like it had been placed there by some kind of evil hand.

Oh, my God, Mama, what happened? He knelt beside her.

Her head came up off the floor and she looked at him.

I'm right here, Mama. It's me. How long you been like this?

I can't half see.

I'll get your glasses.

My Lord, gracious. Where was you at, son?

I was fishing. You know that.

Did you catch anything?

A few bream. Little ones.

Call Dr. Boone.

They don't make house calls anymore, Mama. I'll have to take you to the emergency room.

No, call the ambulance, then call Dr. Boone. He can meet me at the hospital, maybe. Bring me some water. Please. Lord, I couldn't see the dial on the phone. I couldn't find my glasses, and then the phone wouldn't work at all.

I'll be right back, said Flash. He started to leave.

She groaned. He turned back, but didn't kneel. She was confused or something. He hurried to the kitchen, trying to ignore the groaning, and noticed the phone on the floor in the dining room, off the hook. He pressed the button, got a dial tone, and called the operator, who connected him with emergency. He asked them to send an ambulance.

Then he didn't know what to do. He wanted to get his mother off the floor, but he remembered that rule about not moving injured people. He needed to get her glasses for her. He wanted her to stop groaning. For crying out loud, Jesus.

Her glasses were right there under the little ladder. One of the lenses was crushed, pieces of glass on the floor and in the frame. He held the glasses over the trash can and shook them good, then opened a drawer, got a spoon, and cleaned the glass out of the frame. *Thank God the bone hadn't broken through. She could have bled to death.* Maybe it had broken through, but he hadn't seen any blood. He poured a glass of water.

Flash, she called.

I'm coming, Mama. Her head was back down and she was quiet. Here, Mama. Here's some water.

She tried to raise her head. He put his hand under it. It was like a little animal's head. He felt the strands of thin hair. She groaned a little again. He wondered how long she'd been on the floor. *By God, she'd crawled from the kitchen to the bedroom. Why the hell did she do that?*

Why'd you come back here, Mama? You crawled?

I had to go somewhere. I couldn't just sit in the

kitchen. Now I can't even sit up, I don't think. My leg is messed up.

She thought about all those people in the backyard trying to get in. That big crowd. Had she imagined that? Were they angels?

It's broke, Mama. It's flat broke is what it is.

She stayed for three nights at Whittier General. Flash rolled her down to the TV room to watch the Bobby Lee Reese show Saturday night. Her leg was propped out level in a big, white cast. Dr. Boone said she could go home but she would be in a wheelchair for a while.

Flash asked Dwayne's daddy for a half day off to get his mama situated back at home. Dwayne's daddy told him to take his time. To take all the time he needed.

At about noontime on that first day home from the hospital, with his mama in a wheelchair, Flash got to thinking about how he was going to manage. It was clear to him that he needed some help.

He had rolled his mama up to the kitchen table. The arms of the wheelchair wouldn't quite fit under the table, so he'd had to get the dining room table leaf and put that across the wheelchair arms to hold her plate and glass. Mama, Flash said, we got to hire somebody to help out so I can get back to work in a few days. I was thinking we could get Aunt Marzie.

She looked up at him. No. No, sir. We can eat banana sandwiches till I can walk, and I don't...I don't mind a little dust.

It's going to be six weeks in that cast, Mama. I don't want six weeks' worth of banana sandwiches.

You can learn to cook.

I got a job, Mama.

I know that. Well, let's see. Bernice Ingram just went in the County Home and Maybelle Thompson was living with her, so maybe Maybelle is who we need to ask, if we got to ask somebody. She lives with her daughter. Her name is Ivy and her husband is Manley, and he's in the phone book, I'd think. Manley Dees, Maybelle's son-in-law.

Flash called Maybelle Thompson right away.

On the phone, Maybelle said, I'd be happy to meet for an interview. But I'm careful who I work for.

An interview? said Flash.

Well, I don't want to take on nobody without finding out what I'm in for. I mean, I know your mama, know *of* her anyway, used to know some of her people, but not to put too fine a point on it, I ain't never been in your house, and so I'm—

I just need somebody to cook a few meals and do things Mama would do if she didn't have no cast.

What happened?

She fell off a little stepladder.

A little stepladder?

Well, it won't too little. One of them about waist high.

She was up on it?

Flash thought, *Well, hell, yeah — it's kind of hard to fall off something you ain't up on.* Yes, ma'am, she was up on it.

You-all still live across from Jesse Dillworth's store, don't you?

Yes, ma'am.

Well, I'll drive over and look at things.

That's fine. Real fine.

I'll be there tomorrow afternoon.

We'll be right here.

Flash stood waiting for Mrs. Thompson on the porch. He had cut the grass. He wanted it to look good for Mrs. Thompson. He wanted everything to look good for Mrs. Thompson and for this interview she wanted. His mama usually cut the grass, even though she was seventy-four years old, because she said *he* didn't get close enough around the trees and up behind the garage.

He opened Maybelle Thompson's car door for her. He was hoping she'd say yes right away. How you doing, Mrs. Thompson?

Mrs. Thompson leaned on her black wooden cane, a gold-painted ball on top, it looked like. Oh, fine, she said, eyeing the house like it was a chair she was about to buy.

As they approached the porch, where his mama was sitting in her wheelchair with the cast propped up in another chair, Maybelle said, Hey there, Mrs. Acres. I'm sorry to hear about that broke leg.

Well, thank you. It was a bad break. Bone won't just broke. It was shattered. Shattered to bits.

Well, be thankful you didn't get your toes cut off. That's what I'm living with. And believe me, they don't grow back. Like a bone does.

Well a bone don't exactly grow back—if it's been shattered.

Well, you know what I mean. Or you would if you were minus four toes.

You lost some toes?

Four.

How'd that happen?

Lawn mower. I don't like to think about it.

Why'd you bring it up? Flash thought. He had a notion that his mama and Mrs. Thompson might not get along, but he had to hire somebody quick. Her.

I just want to look through your house, Maybelle said to Flash's Mama, because I'm expecting several job offers—one at the County Home, probably—and I want to be happy wherever I settle into. Don't take me as picky. I don't want to be picky, because I got picky people in my family and I know what it's like to put up with picky.

I'm not going to need nobody full time, said Flash's Mama. She had leaned forward some in her wheelchair.

Full-time is the only way I work, said Maybelle Thompson.

Flash wanted somebody full-time. Coming up the steps behind Mrs. Thompson, he said, Mama, let me just...I'm just gone show Mrs. Thompson through the house a minute.

You can call me Maybelle. I ain't that old. I'm old. But I ain't that old. She laughed a laugh Flash thought was too loud.

Inside, they stood in the small hall.

This here's her room and that's my room, said Flash. We just got two bedrooms.

I'd have to stay in your room so I could hear her in the night.

Ma'am?

I'd have to stay in your room so I could hear her in the night.

I wouldn't mind coming to pick you up in the morning and taking you home after supper.

Well, I ain't able to do a lot of moving around from place to place with my toes gone, but I can stay situated in one place pretty well. You could sleep on the couch for a few weeks, couldn't you? I live pretty far out.

Well, I guess, but let me ask you this. He thought, *This is a good sign. She's considering it.* He asked, How much do you charge?

I charge whatever you can pay beyond room and board. My purpose in life is to help people that can't help theirselves. Room and board is all I really need, but I do have a savings account that I like to keep up. I'll tell you the truth, son. What's your name again?

Flash.

I'll tell you the truth, Flash. I can't stand my son-in-law. I love him, but I don't like him. And they don't have nowhere to live except with me. I just relish getting out and helping somebody all I can. It's my calling.

Well, me and Mama already figured out that we could pay you forty cents a hour for a eight-hour day. If that's all right.

As long as the room and board is throwed in, that's fine.

Damn, thought Flash. *Why didn't I say a quarter?*

What I'll be able to do, she said, is fix cereal for

breakfast, and I can cook eggs once in a while and most anything else you got on hand, and I'd appreciate being able to fix something every other night with enough for leftovers for the next day. I ain't ever been one for cooking every day. And can your mother wipe herself all right?

Oh, yeah, she can wipe herself.

Get up and down off the pot?

Oh, yes, ma'am. She holds to the sink to pull herself up.

I knowed a woman pulled a sink outen the wall doing that. 'Course she was considerably larger than your mama. It took about nine people to get her up outen the floor and out of this little-bitty bathroom she was in. Will you be coming home for lunch every day?

Yes, ma'am, that's what I usually do. I usually have a bowl of soup and a sandwich.

You wouldn't be against eating leftovers every other day, would you?

Oh, I'd eat leftovers *every* day.

Do you all like sausage?

Flash wondered what the answer was supposed to be. Do *you?* he asked.

Oh, yes.

We do too. We love it.

When I get a load of wash done, if you could help me hang that out at lunch, I'd appreciate it because with my missing toes I'm not good for standing too long a spell.

I can do that, said Flash. I can change the points and plugs on your car too, he said. Change the oil. Stuff like that.

Late that afternoon, Maybelle moved into Flash's room. He didn't have a lot in there. A dresser, a chair, and a bed. Maybelle placed her open suitcase on the chair, a paper shopping bag with odds and ends on the floor, and her clock and hairbrush on the dresser. She put her toothbrush and toothpaste in the bathroom. She told Flash that her daughter would bring her other things later on.

Flash slept on the couch that night.

The next morning, with all three of them together, Flash felt odd sitting at the kitchen table with his mama while somebody else was standing up cooking eggs. He stood up and said, I'll fix some cereal. Mama eats Corn Flakes and I like Rice Krispies.

Oh, you eat eggs *and* cereal?

Yes, ma'am.

I always just do one or the other.

Well, we do both, said Flash, most of the time.

Flash's Mama said to Maybelle, I'm just glad you ain't a... you know. I'm glad you're white.

Well, me too, said Maybelle. I'm thankful to the Good Lord for so many things in life. I don't have much to complain about at all.

Flash thought about Aunt Marzie. She would have been cheaper. And wouldn't have talked so much.

Except my toes, said Maybelle.

20

For several nights in a row, Dwayne practiced in the mirror while the tape played and he sang along. He'd sing the falsetto while eyeing himself, his head back. He wanted his blood vessels to stand out on his neck, and sometimes they did.

While setting up for practice one Saturday afternoon, Mickey Dean mentioned the Bobby Lee Reese show to Dwayne—were they still going to do the country music and chicken dancing?

Yeah, I want to do that, but we're getting this album down and it's hard to change over to that, but—

It'd be fun to be on TV.

Yeah. We'll do it. I just got to find out when Flash is going to audition.

Okay, said Dwayne to all the boys, I'm going to run this tape ahead. Listen to this. Okay, right here, right about number four twenty-eight. Okay, listen to this where the Flames are saying "I don't mind." They say "I-on-my" real fast. I mean *real* fast. Listen.

They all listened. Willy tried it, laughed, tried it again.

Now, said Dwayne, when we do that, you and Darren have got to sing it like that. Real quick: *I-on-my. I-on-my.* In harmony. I want to get this just like the album and then record it and listen and see how close we got.

My dick itchy, said Willy.

Come on, man. We ain't gone learn nothing like this. Come on.

Mickey Dean said, Why don't we just work on the first song a little bit.

Yeah, let's just play some songs, said Willy. He sat on the arm of the red couch, his electric bass propped straight up on his knee.

There was not a lot of space for maneuvering in the shop room, though each boy had his place to stand. Dwayne had moved a table, legs up, onto the top of another table so he'd have room to dance. They stood facing the door to the refinishing room, where Larry Lime and Flash were working.

Flash ran a smoothing rag over a chair. He asked Larry Lime, What's that name they calling theirselves?

The Amazing Rumblers.

That's what I thought. The Amazing . . . Fumblers is more like it.

Dwayne came into the big room to get water from the water cooler, the black cape over his shoulders.

Larry Lime looked up from his sanding, said to Dwayne, Donnie is missing the beat on that Peter Gunn thing.

How so?

He going like this. Larry Lime sang the notes and slapped his knee, then said, He doing straight two and four. It ought to be like this, he said, so that he hit two and a *half* and four. It makes a big difference. See? Listen.

Why don't you go in and show him.

Naw. That's okay. You can show him.

Okay. Like this?

That's right. You got it right. Then you speed it up like this, see, but he ain't doing that. That's what —

You don't need all that mumbo jumbo shit in there, said Flash.

Larry Lime looked at Flash, then at Dwayne.

Back in the storage room, Dwayne showed Donnie. They practiced. Donnie got it.

Let's try "Please, Please, Please," said Dwayne. That's where I'm going to fall on stage with the cape and everything.

Where?

My dick itchy.

Shut up, Willy, said Gaston.

My dick itchy too, said Ray.

Everybody laughed except James Brown.

Out front of the shop, Larry Lime got into the refrigerated truck with Uncle Young. They were headed to Flint Springs for the meat run.

They're playing James Brown in there, Larry Lime said.

James Brown?

Live at the Apollo.

Kiss my ass.

We going to do all those key changes? Ray asked Dwayne. That sounds like a bunch of key changes.

I got them written down right here, said Dwayne. It's not that hard.

For Donnie, the entire presentation, the sequence, the break song, the introduction leading into "I'll Go Crazy" were all falling together in his head, and he was finding the syncopation he'd missed.

Okay, said Mickey Dean, it works from D all the way up, just a fret at a time or a step at a time, a big chord after he says the name of each song till you get all the way up to B, and then there's this little break and they start playing. And there's got to be a drum hit on the back of each one of those chords...Hear that?...Donnie, can you do that? It kind of frumps it off there.

I can do that, said Donnie.

I'll give you the signal to come in on that Peter Gunn thing right after "James Brown and the Famous Flames," said Darren. I can just drop my arm.

And the second time through, said Dwayne, is where you can hear him come out on stage, so that's where I'll come out with the cape and all.

They listened, practiced, listened, practiced.

It was time for James Brown to sing.

Dwayne held the mic to his mouth, head back. You know, I feel awwwwwright. You know, I feel awright, chil'ren. I feel awwwaaawwwwawright. He drew his shoulders in a bit; he didn't want to seem quite so tall and lanky, quite so white. He was making a sound like the screeching of wild things. He dropped his arm for the music intro, lifted his left foot, walked to his left on his right foot — heel-toe, heel-toe — while the band practiced.

21

RAY WHEELER: *Do you remember the Bleeder?*

BOBBY LEE REESE: *Oh, yeah. He was teaching a black kid from across the tracks. He was an incredible guitar player. Baby Mercy and I would go to hear him play with that group he played with at the Frog. A jazz group.*

Way, way back, I spent some time across the tracks doing research for my honors thesis from Ballard about the Fitzsimmons plantation, and I got to know some people. Went to church over there a couple times.

I can tell you about my audience on both sides of

the track, if you allow some generalizing. Did you ever visit across the tracks?

RAY WHEELER: *I never went in any houses.*

BOBBY LEE REESE: *Around living rooms over there, just like on our side, besides a big old TV cabinet, you'd find ceramic bluebirds and/or ceramic bird dogs, maybe a ceramic chicken, a framed marriage picture or two, a picture of somebody in his U.S. service uniform, little framed photos of family members on tables, or maybe on a wall — some taken at school by a yearbook photographer. In East Starke, as you know, you might see a Sears catalog or* Boys Life. *Two Bibles or more per house on either side. Doilies on couch arms.*

Sometimes four or six Bibles in a family, handed down. All King James's. But this ain't why you're here, is it?

RAY WHEELER: *Well, no, not exactly.*

BOBBY LEE REESE: *Sometimes when I think back on those Amazing Rumblers, I think about what all was coming up in the mad late sixties. And this sudden appearance of black-white dance clubs all around that part of North Carolina, at least three or four, and that jazz club up in Whittier that the Bleeder eventually moved to. But that was in the late sixties. You're here to talk about the show, right?*

RAY WHEELER: *Right.*

22

ONCE THE CAST was off and Flash's Mama learned to get around using two canes, Maybelle got her in her car and took her up to the Hallstons' for Sunday dinner. Maybelle was slated to go home the next day.

Around the table were Dwayne, his father and mother—Marcus and Swansee—Maybelle, and Flash's Mama.

Well, it just so happened, said Flash's Mama, that Flash auditioned on the worst night of all because there was this woman auditioning who's already been to Nashville and made a record, and of course they picked her. Sharon Van Horn. She was about as much a amateur as I'm a . . . a fish. She was Miss Summerlin a few years ago too. Of course if I'd a knowed that *she* was going to be auditioning, I'd a told Flash not to audition because God knows they get somebody on there like her with a figure-eight shape and able to sing or *not*, she's going to win *any* audition. It won't Bobby Lee that give Flash the thumbs down, it was that Jared Fitzsimmons. That's what Flash said. He also said that Sharon Van Horn was all over Fitzsimmons after the audition. Nothing surprises me anymore. I'm glad I ain't met him. Owns everything in Hanson County, as you know. Plus them one-legged dolls.

Flash's Mama removed her glasses, rubbed her eyes, put her glasses back on.

A community rumor was that Fitzsimmons kept a small house of one-legged dolls because of his sister. She was born with only one leg and died, and people said he kept the dolls in an old house near the plantation site and made Young Jones take presents to them every Christmas.

Flash's Mama continued talking. Flash didn't have a chainst and now he can't audition for at least another year, and he's got a wonderful voice. I'll bet you Bobby Lee wanted him in. You should hear him, Maybelle. Marcus and Swansee, y'all have heard him out there in the shop. He kept his guitar in there for a while, I think. Dwayne, you've heard him, ain't you?

Oh, yeah.

I think he got worried about the guitar getting stolen, with…you know. Could you pass those string beans? Did you put a little sugar in them, Swansee?

Just a touch of vinegar.

After dinner, Maybelle and Flash's Mama and the rest had moved to the big front porch — four rockers, a wooden swing, and steps with black, metal rails. Dwayne sat on the steps. They were eating watermelon.

Flash's Mama sat in the swing. Well, they've started burning up dead people around here now, she said. Somebody at the church's cousin had it in her will that she wanted that cremation after she died.

Well, I'd hope it'd be after she died, said Maybelle. I never understood that stuff. I just wouldn't want to take a chance about being raised from the dead.

I do wonder about the second coming, too, said Flash's Mama. It does seem like it would be easier and more normal to get raised from the dead when you're buried in one piece.

Dwayne's daddy stared at Flash's Mama.

Dwayne sat with his back against the step railing, looking up at the others. He said, What about when someone's been underground so long they're nothing but dust?

Well, that would be *dust*, said Maybelle. Dust is lots closer to a human body than ashes. Dust is natural — a natural ingredient, more or less.

That's right, said Flash's Mama. You just don't ever know anymore about the habits of society. The world is changing so fast. You used to could predict things. But not anymore, especially with a Catholic president.

And the Cubans trying to bomb us, said Maybelle.

Life goes on, said Dwayne's father.

Ain't it the truth, said Flash's Mama. Ain't it the truth. And I'm glad we got Bobby Lee Reese on TV. I'd say about all we need on TV is Billy Graham and Bobby Lee Reese. And I'll tell you this. Flash will audition again in a year. I'll see to it. And I'll meet Jared Fitzsimmons sometime between now and then and give him a piece of my mind about that Sharon Van Horn.

I wouldn't be surprised, said Maybelle, if Bobby Lee don't become a national star. I've heard say he's headed to Nashville.

That would be something, wouldn't it? said Flash's Mama. Somebody from so near Starke. I just wish Flash could have got on there.

My band's going to try to get on Bobby Lee's show with a dancing chicken, said Dwayne.

A dancing chicken? said Flash's Mama. Where in the world would you get a dancing chicken?

Larry Lime Nolan. He trained one.

Oh. Well, I ain't surprised.

23

Dwayne, awake in the middle of the night, going to the bathroom because of too much watermelon, heard a train whistle from far north. The night was quiet and the sound faint.

He heard the whistle again, louder, with an echo this time. He climbed back into bed. In a few minutes he'd be able to hear the loud rumble and clanging, the horn blasting before the North Cut and then before the South Cut. Sometimes a conductor used a soft touch and released short, quiet toots—not the full-force blast—or a full, long one and two shorts, or two longs. Dwayne visualized the conductor pulling a hanging cord like the ones truck drivers pulled. Or maybe he pressed a button.

*   *   *

A few minutes earlier, Larry Lime had been awakened by loud squawkings in the backyard. He wondered if the chickens were fighting. Then he decided something must be in the pen, something bad. Coon, possum, dog. He pulled on blue jeans, shoes, and his orange T-shirt. He grabbed a flashlight from the kitchen and the .22 rifle from over the back door. It would be loaded.

As he walked to the chicken pen he heard the same distant train whistle that Dwayne was hearing. He kept the flashlight off because the moon was bright. He heard but didn't register the rumble of the train, a quiet, far-off, steady thunder. He stood at the door to the chicken pen. Feathers were scattered near the gate. He couldn't tell their color in the moonlight. He turned on the flashlight. Redbird. There was a hole pushed through the chicken wire just by the door. He shined the light around. He walked toward the woods but didn't see her anywhere. The whistle was a deep-throated, powerful sound — at the North Cut. He heard the airy *ch* at the beginning of the sound, making it thick and rich. Months ago he'd noticed that the sound had several tones in it — four? five? — but he'd been unable to figure the intervals. He shined the light into the woods. Slowly to the left, to the right. There. He

walked to the spot and looked at what was left of Redbird. A possum did it. The powerful blast of sound
echoed all through the woods and off houses as if he
were standing in the Grand Canyon.

At his house, Dwayne wondered about how such a
loud noise wouldn't wake him at night, wouldn't wake
all the people in Starke who, like him, had become
accustomed to the sound.

After school the next day, at Larry Lime's house, Redbird lay in a large cardboard box by the back door. Izzy
and Bethany sat on the back steps crying.

Booker walked into the kitchen from the bedroom.
His size seemed to shrink the small kitchen.

What's wrong with them? he asked.

Something got Redbird last night, said Canary.
Larry Lime said a possum.

Booker picked up a biscuit off the table. I ain't
surprised.

Canary said, Izzy and Bethany saw her this morning and starting crying, and I promised them a funeral.
That's the way it ought to be. Canary leaned back
against the sink. On the walls around her were open
cabinets, no cabinet doors.

Booker turned, walked to the back door, looked at
the chicken. Where's Larry Lime?

He ought to be home in a minute. He said he wanted to bury her.

We'll eat her. She ain't much damaged.

We can't eat Redbird, Booker.

Why not? He sat at the kitchen table.

'Cause she was a pet. You wouldn't eat Scrap.

Scrap's a dog. Was Scrap here when the possum come? said Booker. Something run off that possum.

I don't know.

Booker looked around. They got to shut up that crying, he said. We can eat her along with another chicken. Not know which is which. Fry them together.

No.

You could be eating a leg and not know which is which.

Booker, that wouldn't make it any better.

I'll eat her, he said.

We have to have a funeral for the children.

Give her to Aunt Marzie. She can do dumplings and give it back to us.

We can dig a grave out back, said Canary. That's the proper thing to do. We need to get beyond it. She looked at the clock on the wall. Larry Lime'll be home in a minute.

At the edge of the garden, Booker began digging the grave. The kids stood close, watching, sniffling.

The cardboard box holding the chicken was about the size of half a refrigerator.

I'll go get something littler to bury her in, said Canary. We need to wait for Larry Lime. She went in the house and came back out with a shoe box. At the grave, she opened it, and measured with her eyes. Too small, she said.

I could tole you that, said Booker. Get that towel on the back porch, or some kind of old rag.

Larry Lime walked up, came over, and looked in. Redbird lay on her side.

Larry Lime imagined Redbird dancing. He saw her following him around the yard. She wouldn't follow anybody else; she ate from his hand, climbed into his lap. When she roosted away from the others, he'd lift her on cold nights from the head-high tree limb behind the garage and take her to the chicken pen, holding her under his arm, and with his free hand rub her comb and feel the heat that came from the sides of her head. Then he'd open the chicken pen gate and put her in with the others.

Larry Lime said, That son of a bitch possum.

Larry Lime! said Canary. Don't you talk that way. Don't you ever talk that way. I didn't know you thought words like that. I'll get something to bury her in. She started back in.

Stop crying, Booker said to the little ones. It ain't nothing but a chicken.

I was teaching her to dance, said Larry Lime. I mean, I'd taught her. Some guys were going to get her on TV.

TV? said Booker. Here, finish digging this hole.

Larry Lime took the shovel. She was smart, he said. Now I'll have to teach another one.

Why didn't you teach more than one?

It's easier with one.

Canary was coming across the yard with Booker's mustard-yellow shirt, folded.

The hole was finished. Larry Lime squatted like he'd seen Flash Acres do. Booker saw the shirt. His mouth dropped open.

Sweeties, Canary said to Izzy and Bethany, we're going to bury Redbird in this warm sunshine shirt, and she'll be warm forever and ever.

Wait a minute, said Booker. You—

Canary looked at him.

24

THE PHONE RANG in the refinishing room of the shop. Flash answered.

Flash, this is Maybelle. Your mama's had a stroke. I just came in from the backyard, and she's here in the bed with one side of her face all drawed down, and she can't do nothing but mumble. I called a ambulance. It's the left side that's not working, which means that the stroke is in the right side of her brain. I can't remember what that means, but I think that's the talking side. She's got a significant mumble going on.

As Flash got into his Ford he visualized his mother's face pulled down on one side. He drove the quarter mile home. Walking in the back way through the kitchen, he noticed that the piece of newspaper his mother always kept over the trash can to keep the gnats away, and that Maybelle never remembered to put on, was off, so he picked it up off the floor and put it in place and headed on back to the bedroom.

Mama, he said.

She didn't turn her head toward him. He walked to the far side of the bed, looked at her face. Her eyes were open, but they didn't seem to be working somehow.

For the two weeks that Flash's Mama was in the hospital and Maybelle was back at her own house, Flash, while he was home, fed the birds because his mama would have, and he used paper plates when he wanted to—because his mother wasn't right there to stop him.

He visited her every day. On the second day, he had a talk with Maybelle. Maybelle made it clear that not much could be done but treat her like a baby in diapers—which she would sure enough be in for a while. If not for the duration, Maybelle clarified. This was all leading up to Maybelle telling Flash that her job was to take care of people who were ambulatory.

What's that? asked Flash.

Can get around on their own. Don't you remember me telling you that?

What?

That I could take care of your mama as long as she was ambulatory?

Not exactly. No, I don't think I remember that.

I'm sorry, I don't have no kind of medical certificates that would allow me to meet your mama's needs. I'll help you the first day or two she's home, and then I'll have to excuse myself.

Do you know anybody I could get?

Not right off. You might try some of the colored women from across the tracks.

Mama wouldn't like that.

There's going to be a lot in this final stretch that she don't like. And it *is* a final stretch, and that's something if I was you I wouldn't try to fight. You're young and you work close to your house. You could check on her in the morning, at lunch, and a couple of times in the afternoon.

Mr. Hallston told Flash to take as long as he needed at home, away from the shop, but that he might want to get some help there at home. Flash asked him if he knew where he might get some, and Mr. Hallston said he didn't know—other than Aunt Marzie or some of her people.

And then the day came when a nurse rolled Flash's Mama out to his car and finished up on all she'd taught

Flash by showing him how to get her from the wheelchair into the car passenger seat and back, how to fold
the wheelchair for the car trunk, how to transfer the
urine bag and catheter. The nurse was a large woman
and was able to lock the wheels on the wheelchair, face
Flash's Mama, get her under the arms, turn her and sit
her in the passenger seat of his Ford, and then get her
legs in and the urine bag in — with Flash's Mama's
head kind of hanging while she grabbed at nothing
with her good hand.

The nurse got Flash's Mama out of the car and back
in the wheelchair, and then made Flash load her in
while his mama was trying to say something like "No,
not again, for God's sake," but it didn't come out like
that. It was more like a gargle.

Maybelle was sitting on the small porch when
Flash turned into the driveway. She walked out and
sort of took over, showing Flash how to get his mama
out of the car and into the wheelchair.

Flash said, That's not the way they showed me at
the hospital.

There's more'n one way to skin a horse, said
Maybelle.

They got her inside and in the bed, finally.

The nurse had told Flash it was very important to
write down how much his mother urinated each eight

hours, that it should be at least seven ounces, as measured right there on the bag, and if it was less than that, then she needed more water. She told him to check the general condition of the pee in the bag and to not empty it before eight hours so he could keep up with the amount.

He'd learned to take her blood pressure.

Later, he had all her medications together on her dresser.

Did they show you at the hospital about changing her diaper? asked Maybelle.

Yeah, roll her way over and all that. Way over. I've done it a couple of times, and I've got to get her some baby food. The one with bananas. She likes bananas, but she won't eat much and I ain't tried to put her teeth in yet. Could you, ah...

Yeah, I'll help you with that.

It's a couple of partial bridges. One up, one down.

I'll get her something to eat in a minute, said Maybelle.

I was going to give her some applesauce. Maybe a banana sandwich if her teeth are in. The bridges are in a glass of water in the bathroom. I'll get them.

Flash set the glass on the bedside table, got the bridges out with his fingers, dried them with toilet paper, leaving some paper stuck on.

Okay, Mama, we're going to put your teeth in.

Flash's Mama rolled her head toward Flash, seemed to recognize him. Her front two teeth rested on her upper lip. He held the upper bridge — six teeth on a metal frame — about five inches in front of his mother's eyes.

You want me to help you? asked Maybelle.

No, that's okay. I'll do it. Here. Here they come, Mama. Open up.

She opened her mouth, and he slipped the bridge in and arranged and pressed while his mother's head moved with the pressure. She frowned and kind of glared. The bridge snapped into place.

The bottom one had only four teeth. Flash studied it for a few seconds and popped that one in more easily. Oh, I see, he said.

Now you can do it all, said Maybelle, and I can get on the road.

You can't stay tonight?

I've already got another client.

That night, before bed, Flash asked, Mama, when I get your bridges out you want me to brush your teeth for you?

Brush my . . . teeth.

She spoke! She spoke! He wanted to tell somebody. He needed somebody there.

Okay, Mama. You just talked. That's good. Now here goes. He managed to get her bridges out while she glared up at him. He took them to the bathroom, filled her glass with fresh water, and dropped in her teeth. He was soon back with her toothbrush with toothpaste on it. He held a pan beneath her chin. She grabbed the brush and brushed her two front teeth.

Okay, Mama, spit in the pan.

She spit hard, over the pan and onto her pajama shirt, pants, and him.

Mama, you overdone it.

She was trying to tell him something. Lillerine, she said.

You want Listerine?

She nodded. She was getting better already. She was recovering quickly. He found the Listerine, held it to her lips. She helped him tilt the bottle up, down; then she swallowed.

Mama! You don't drink Listerine.

She was frowning.

See, you don't drink it. You rinse. You rinse.

She was still frowning.

Just rinse, he said.

She tried again, drank another mouthful.

Mama. Damn it. I'm putting this up. You're not supposed to drink it. Jesus.

In the bathroom, Flash said to himself, I need some help.

Back at her side, he said, Mama, I'm going to get some help. I got to. Maybelle done flew the coop.

Later, settled in his bed, he listened for her to make a sound. Just as he was drifting off, he heard her call his name, as clear as a bell. He got up and, in her room, found her crossways on the bed. Her sheet and blanket were somehow balled underneath her.

Mama, what are you doing?

Don't you tell nobody I did this.

He was astonished. *A clear sentence.* That's good, Mama, he said. You're talking!

She tried to speak again. He couldn't understand her. It sounded like "jarman, jarman."

Mama, you just said, "Don't tell nobody." Can you say that again? Can you say "don't"?

Jarman. She frowned.

I don't know what you're saying. You were just talking. Talk again.

She turned her head away from him.

He managed to get her back straight in the bed. He slipped his finger into her diaper like the nurse had taught him. She was dry. Clean.

*　　*　　*

The next morning Flash changed his mother's diaper, put a couch cushion and two pillows behind her back, got her sitting up, and then fed her some cereal, Corn Flakes. She ate half a bowl.

He was proud of his success, but he needed to be at the shop doing some overtime work. It was Saturday. Mama, I'm going to call Mr. Hallston. I got to get some help. I got to get Aunt Marzie or Larry Lime's mama, maybe. Just till you start getting better. They ain't gone do nothing but dirty work.

She was playing with the sheet like she was trying to fold it. She wasn't listening to him.

He phoned Mr. Hallston, but the line was busy. He came back to her room, and she was trying to fold the sheet again. He went to the kitchen and got four clean, folded kitchen rags, came back and put them in her lap.

She looked at them.

Mama, if you got to fold something, why don't you fold something that will fold. You can't get that whole sheet folded unless you stand up with somebody to help out.

Flash went back to the kitchen, got Mr. Hallston on the phone, explained the situation. Mr. Hallston agreed to check with Aunt Marzie and Larry Lime's mother.

When he got to her bed, his mother was trying again to fold the sheet. He started to the kitchen to fix himself something to eat.

She moaned loudly. He came back to her. She was frowning, looking at the ceiling.

Where does it hurt, Mama?...Mama, can you tell me where it hurts? It looked like the right side of her face had dropped down some more, somehow. Mama? Mama?

She spit onto her pajama shirt.

You sure as hell ain't forgot how to spit.

He heard a crow outside, and another bird singing.

This afternoon, he said, we'll get you up in that wheelchair.

Aunt Marzie was helping shell peas at Canary's house. They were sitting on the front porch. It was hot. Izzy and Bethany were in the backyard playing marbles. Aunt Marzie was telling Canary that Mrs. Acres, across from the Bone Store, had had a serious stroke, that Flash had been talking to Mr. Hallston on the phone about getting help, and that Mr. Hallston wondered if she or Canary might help out. And, said Aunt Marzie, I ain't gone have time to do more'n a very little bit, and I'll tell you this: I'll have to pray hard to the Good Lord that I don't inflict some kind of poison in that lady's orange juice. That's what I'll have to pray for. Do you know what she ast me at the store one time?

Oh, yes, said Canary. You told me. *More than once,* she thought.

I was getting something for Mrs. Hallston, and they was talking about that dog-food-eating fool on the TV, and she —

You done told me, Aunt Marzie.

She said to me, "You people eat dog food outen the can, don't you?"

Yeah, I know about that, said Canary. She said lots of other stuff too, and so has her son, Flashy-Ass.

Well, said Aunt Marzie, it be might hard for me to *serve* her instead of *service* her with some kind of mischief. Put some more peas in there.

She can't talk much can she?

That's what they say.

I got a idea, said Canary. I just got this funny idea. You know about that meat run last week?

No.

The truck broke down and a whole load of meat got spoiled.

Really?

It was awful. Awful. The generator thing that keep the refrigerated part of the truck going broke down, so Young and Larry Lime got back late, and all us at the freezer room done gone home cause we didn't think he was coming in at all. He got in and parked the truck after we left, 'cause he didn't want to wake nobody up with a phone call, and then next morning he got over there, and it was a real hot night, see, and what's happening is on the back bumper of that truck is a big glob of maggots already dripping out from the inside that truck, and the smell is beyond the worst thing you—

That's enough, said Aunt Marzie.

Wait. Wait for my idea I just had. Anyway, Mr. Fitzsimmons, he would a went through the roof if Young called late at night, and Young figured the meat once spoiled is going to stay spoiled, 'cause, see, Young done called him about something else one night and Mr. Fitzsimmons say, "Don't you ever call me about nothing in the night no more, you hear me?" and so Young ain't about to call him. Anyway, listen. Listen. They take the truck to the dump and it's on the scales, see, and the man come out with a clipboard and he say this—he standing there at the driver's window and he say, "So, okay, what you got?" And Young, he say, "We got some meat we need to dump," and the man say,

"Meat? What kind of meat?" And Young say, "Oh, just some meat what got hot," and the man start walking back toward the back of the truck, and there's these weep holes, see, in the back corners of the truck for stuff to drip out, and Young look back in the rearview mirror, and there's this black liquid a-dripping out the weep holes, and before the man get back there he done throwed up on his clipboard because, honey, there's about a thousand pounds of spoiled livers and lungs in there. And so the man made them take that stuff over to the back side of the dump where the wind—

That's enough.

—where the wind don't even blow, and there's these deep holes they had to throw that meat into wid pitchforks—you ought to hear Larry Lime talk about it—so they can run a bulldozer over there to cover it up.

Now my plan, said Canary, don't involve no meat, but listen...

In the back room at the shop, the Amazing Rumblers practiced.

Flash sat in the bedroom looking at his mother. He had it all straight about the catheter and the urine bag and how to get her up into her wheelchair, but he was tired, thinking he'd wait another day to get her up. In the meantime, he needed help.

The Bleeder sat on the couch in his house trailer. He reread a letter he got in the mail that day. He was being invited to play weekly at a jazz club in Whittier — a new club. Money was involved. Good money.

25

WHEN CANARY CAME to work at Flash's Mama's on Monday morning, Flash gave instructions about the urine bag, when to empty it, what to write down where, and then he showed her, with his arms wrapped around his mama, how to get her up out of the bed and into the wheelchair. She grunted and he grunted. His mother eyed Canary with alarm. Flash found it was harder getting her up and down than he thought it would be. He worked up a sweat in the hot bedroom. He didn't let Canary practice.

I'm going to roll her down the hall to the kitchen table, he said, and let you fix her some cereal and see if she'll eat it. How much you going to charge to help us out?

How about sixty-five cents an hour?

That's a little high. I can do forty-five.

I don't know.

I'll give Larry Lime some breaks at work.

Flash was rolling his mother, now in the wheel-chair, out of the bedroom and into the hallway. Her head moved as if she had no balance. Canary was behind him.

Maybe I can do fifty, said Flash.

Flash's Mama straightened her left side like she was stretching and pulled her head back like she was in some kind of a painful trance. She seemed stiff enough to break. She started crying, then cried out, God, let me die. Oh, God, let me die.

Flash was still sweating hard from getting her into the wheelchair. Sweat was dripping off the end of his nose. He looked down on her unwashed head, the thin hair spinning out from that cowlick in the crown.

Damn, he said. She's feeling pretty bad. Mama, Mama. Don't say that. Don't you say that. That's not nice. You're getting better. You hear? Then to Canary he said, You think you can get her back in the bed after breakfast? I got to go to work.

I'm sure I can.

How about fifty cents an hour and I'll take care of Larry Lime at work. Give him some time off. With pay. Something like that.

That'll do okay.

When he got his mother's wheelchair up against the kitchen table with the table leaf over her lap, he said to Canary, Maybe you can fix me a bowl of cereal too. Me and her. I had somebody to do all this before Mama had her stroke, but she flew the coop.

Aunt Marzie is working at Donnie's Mama's house. She decides to take her lunch break early — take her wrapped sandwich down to Flash's Mama's to do Canary's little plan. She tells Donnie's Mama that she'll be back directly. She smiles as she walks down the road.

Aunt Marzie gets Flash's Mama's Bible from the living room, walks into the bedroom, and says, Canary, why don't you take a break and go on out and sit on the porch a minute. I got a notion to read some from the book of Psalms.

Yessum.

Canary leaves.

Aunt Marzie says, I'm gone sit right here, Mrs. Acres, and read you some from Psalms. You listen up now. Here we go. Dis here is the twenty-third Psalm. "The Lord is my Shepherd; I shall not want. He maketh me lie down in green pastures." And, she says, a bunch of cows is all out there in the green pastures, and the shepherds are mean so they cut the insides out of them cows, and it all plop out on the ground and bubble up.

Flash's Mama, frowning, cuts her eyes to Aunt Marzie.

Aunt Marzie looks up from the Bible, and the two women are locked into each other for a few seconds.

Then Aunt Marzie says, Why, you ain't nothing but a poor ole, sick white woman without your mouth. I done missed my chance to trouble you. She looks down. "He leadeth me beside the still waters. He restoreth my soul." But she wants to say, "And wait till you hear about what happen to all that pretty pink meat, how it turned blue, then green, then dark green." But she doesn't. She finishes her reading, "And I will dwell in the House of the Lord forever."

She hears a car drive up. She says, You-all afraid if we take over we might treat y'all like you treated us. And you might be right.

Flash walks into the bedroom. Hey, Mama. She looks a little upset, he says. Is she okay? He looks at Aunt Marzie, sitting with the Bible open in her lap.

She fine, says Aunt Marzie. I been reading to her out the Good Book.

26

BOBBY LEE REESE: *Thursday evenings at six thirty, under the tent behind the TV-station parking lot was when and where we had the auditions for the amateur acts. Inside in the winter. We had some doozy acts, and some really bad acts. But there was an energy about those auditions, a kind of urgency and feeling about luck and fortune and defeat all hanging in the air.*

Let's see, on that particular Thursday, it was a cool fall evening. I remember the Rumblers driving up in a hearse. The Amazing Rumblers. They had it written somehow on the side of this big, black Cadillac hearse. They were a — you-all were an enthusiastic bunch of boys.

RAY WHEELER: *I was the first one who got there. I wadn't in the hearse. I was driving my daddy's DeSoto. Then the other guys came in the Cadillac. I remember seeing Baby Mercy under the tent, behind a table, with her white hat on — I had a crush on her. One of those TV crushes kind of like I got on Annette Funicello, Mickey Mouse Club. But I'd never seen Baby Mercy up close, and I'm sure before the night was over she knew I had a crush on her because I got to talk to her a little bit. And I remember you had on a white shirt, loose at the collar — unbuttoned an extra button hole down the front, I remember for some reason.*

BOBBY LEE REESE: *Wearing a gold chain, probably. You probably remember that audition better than I do.*

RAY WHEELER: *I remember the chain because it kind of surprised me. I never saw it on TV. A producer, I think, was there behind the table. And some other people from the show. And Jared Fitzsimmons.*

BOBBY LEE REESE: *He'd come every once in a while. I remember thinking how young you guys were and then you were about halfway through "Hey Good*

Lookin' " and I stood up because as far as I was concerned it was all over. You all had it.

RAY WHEELER: *I remember you asked us if we could do a second song, and Dwayne said, "I Saw the Light." But I need to ask you some general questions about the show before we get back to that.*

27

FRIDAY AFTERNOON, after work, Dwayne was shooting basketball with Larry Lime at the new hoop out behind his house—between the shop and his backyard. The band had auditioned successfully, and Dwayne was telling Larry Lime about the Amazing Rumblers being on Bobby Lee's show the next night. In the days since Redbird's death, Larry Lime had tried to train another chicken but didn't have the luck he had with Redbird. The band would do the show without a chicken.

Dwayne, on some level, knew that he probably shouldn't be shooting basketball with Larry Lime right there in his backyard, but doing so was a little easier since Flash, after stripping a dresser, had gone home to his sick mama. They said she was getting worse. Larry Lime's mama was taking care of her, with help from Aunt Marzie.

Dwayne and Larry Lime were playing horse. If one boy shot a basket, the other had to make the same shot—layup, reverse layup, set shot, jump shot. If he missed, he'd be assigned an *h*. Next miss, an *o*, and so on. First one to get to *horse* lost.

Dwayne's daddy came out of the shop, headed to the house. He stopped, called to Dwayne, Come here a minute.

Dwayne tossed the basketball to Larry Lime and walked up to his father. He thought his father was going to ask him to do something in the shop, something he'd forgotten to do.

His father said, He shouldn't be out here.

What?

You know. It just don't look right.

You mean..., Dwayne turned to look at Larry Lime, dribbling, then shooting a jump shot.

Dwayne's father experienced a few seconds of doubt, but just as he did, just as the doubt—maybe a touch of guilt—began to creep in, the gravity of the historical moment, the fact that negroes were behind some kind of uprising, some kind of impertinence following the likes of Martin Luther King, all that moved into his consciousness and said, yes—yes, in *his* day it would have perhaps been okay, this scene before him, but with them beginning to make a fuss, all that marching and sitting at lunch counters, all that—that uppity behavior: it just was not right, somehow.

You need to ask him to leave, Dwayne's daddy said.

To leave? Dwayne said, looking into his father's face. They were the same height. His father's upper lip was covered in sweat beads.

Now, his father said.

Dwayne walked up to Larry Lime. He looked back at his father, now walking to the back porch, then back at Larry Lime. Dwayne was caught in a vacant place. He didn't know what to say. He said, You know what the Bermuda Triangle is?

Oh, yeah, said Larry Lime.

There's a movie about it at the drive-in. Walk with me to the shop. I got a idea. You want to go? See *The Bermuda Triangle*?

Yeah, but they won't let me in. Whites only.

What if you were...in the car trunk until I drove us in? We could park away from other people, and you could get in the backseat.

When?

Tonight. You got a girlfriend, right?

Yeah, but I ain't sure she'll go.

What's her name?

Olive.

Just before dark, Dwayne pulled the big, white '60 Buick to a stop at the Luther's Chin Road–South Cut intersection. Sitting on the school-bus stop bench was Larry Lime and Olive Creedmoor, his girlfriend. Larry Lime stood, then she stood.

Olive was a little taller than Larry Lime. And older.

Linda, sitting close beside Dwayne, said for the second time, What are you doing? The first time he hadn't answered.

I'm stopping to pick up Larry Lime and his girlfriend.

Why?

They're going with us to the drive-in.

We can't do that.

We can if they get in the trunk.

Dwayne got out of the car and headed for the trunk. Larry Lime stepped over the ditch and onto the road. Olive was still standing in front of the bench — back across the ditch.

Come on, Larry Lime said to her.

You didn't tell me about this, she said, her chin tucked in.

I told you we was going to the movie.

You didn't say who with.

Well, we're going to the movie. The drive-in. *The Bermuda Triangle*. With Dwayne. Larry Lime looked into the car, nodded. And her. We're gone hide in the trunk till we get there.

I ain't going nowhere, said Olive.

All we got to do is get in the trunk.

Are you crazy? I ain't getting in no damn white-ass car trunk with no damn white-ass people to go see no damn white-ass drive-in movie. You crazy. She stood, took a long-legged jump across the ditch, and started walking north along the road.

Larry Lime looked at Dwayne. She'll cool down, he said. She like that. Open the trunk, man. I want to see that scary stuff.

Dwayne opened the trunk. Larry Lime climbed in.

I got a blanket in there, said Dwayne, and a rope so you can tie it almost closed.

Dwayne pulled the car up to the Starlite Drive-In Theater ticket booth not long after sunset. The horizon line was purple, almost time for the projector to turn on. In the popcorn and soda shop—also the projection booth—near the middle of the grounds, live snakes were kept in glass display cases. Alligator purses and shoes were sold. During showtimes, a German shepherd bedded inside by the door.

Dwayne pulled the big Buick too far past the ticket booth, put the automatic transmission into reverse, and backed up to the window. He had no small bills, only the fifty his daddy had paid him for furniture-shop work. He offered it to the lady behind the ticket window.

I can't take a fifty. I just opened the money box. I need my change, honey.

Linda was sitting stiff, looking straight ahead.

I need some change, Dwayne said to Linda.

I can't believe this, she said. She reached for her purse in the floorboard behind the front seat but couldn't find it. Behind them a horn tooted. Linda found her purse. Dwayne paid with her five and got change back. He was in a hurry to get past the window, so he held the steering wheel and stomped on the gas, forgetting the car was in reverse.

After the crash, Dwayne looked at the car behind him, and then over at Linda as he opened his door. She was sitting with her head in her hands. Are you okay? he asked her, as he put his foot on the ground.

I can't believe this, she said.

The guy behind him was out of his car, a '55 Ford. Dwayne had both feet on the ground when the woman at the ticket window, leaning forward, said, Will you pull on through, son? I got to get people in.

Dwayne said to the man, I'm just going to pull forward.

What the hell were you doing? said the man.

I forgot I was in reverse.

Forgot?! Holy Cow.

Dwayne got in behind the steering wheel, started the car, and pulled forward to a spot behind the last row of speakers. He got out, walked around, and looked at the trunk. It was not closed, but the dent was such that Dwayne wasn't sure he could open it. Or close it.

The guy had pulled up his car, stopped, got out.

I'm sorry, Dwayne said.

Have you got people in the trunk? said the guy.

People in the *trunk?* No.

You do too. That trunk was already open. I saw somebody move in there while you were over there at the ticket window.

No, I—

The guy walked back to the ticket booth. He's got somebody in the trunk, he said to the ticket lady.

Dwayne pushed down, pulled up on the trunk lid.

It would go neither way. He bent over, looked into the crack. We in some deep shit, he whispered.

Tell them I'm a spare tire, said Larry Lime.

We in some deep shit.

The guy, walking up, said to Dwayne, You better open that trunk, let whoever's in there out.

The ticket lady walked up.

The trunk won't open, Dwayne said. He looked in at Linda. Her face was still in her hands.

You can try, said the ticket lady.

A car horn sounded back at the ticket booth.

Dwayne thought about getting in the car and calmly driving away, but he visualized those spikes that would rotate up at the exit and pop his tires. No way out. He tried to close the trunk again. It was jammed with only a small crack to see through. He looked at Linda. The same.

Now the guy was beside him, bending over, looking into the trunk. He was bald-headed, kind of old, wearing an armless T-shirt. Dwayne could smell aftershave lotion.

Yep, the guy said, somebody's in there. Somebody's in there, he said to the ticket lady.

A car horn blew again.

I'll get my flashlight, she said.

I'll just pay and leave, said Dwayne. I'll pay you fifty dollars, he said to the ticket woman, now headed back to the ticket booth.

Fifty dollars? she said. I'm damn sure going to look now.

Dwayne looked off the property at a streetlight against the deep purple sky. Bugs were flying around it, like at night baseball games. It was one of those lights that came on by itself.

The woman came back, bent over, and shined the flashlight into the trunk. She stood straight, looked at the other guy. It's a nigger, she said. At least one. I'm calling the law. You better be glad Ralph ain't here. He keeps his German shepherd hungry.

Dwayne looked at the streetlight again. It seemed far, far away. He said, I didn't know anybody was in there. But the woman was walking back to the ticket booth. She hadn't heard him. Dwayne looked at the car trunk, wondered if Larry Lime heard him.

The man said to Dwayne, I need some kind of insurance information. He looked at the front end of his car. Man, your ass is grass. He kneeled to look in the trunk.

It's in the glove compartment, said Dwayne. All you got is a busted headlight. I'm going to be in trouble, sir—could you just call me up later or something? Dwayne felt hot in his chest, up his neck, around his ears. I mean—

You backed into my car, the man said. I need your insurance information.

Dwayne got the insurance card out of the car. Linda's face still rested in her hands. The guy wrote the insurance information down, got in his car, and moved across humps that held up the fronts of cars, on toward the front row, and then he and his girlfriend walked back and watched and waited for the law—just to see what would happen.

Before arriving at the Starlite, Deputy Sheriff Howell, Donnie's daddy, figured that with a negro being in a whites-only establishment, along with all the national negro trouble, the newspaper ought to know, so he called his switchboard and told the deputy on duty to call the editor at the newspaper.

The editor at the *Prestonville Courier-News*, before sending a reporter and photographer, called Jared Fitzsimmons, the paper's owner. This was proof, he told Fitzsimmons, that the Martin Luther King integration business had finally made it to Starke.

Fitzsimmons headed to the drive-in. When he arrived, Deputy Howell had a white boy, a white girl, and a negro standing beside a 1960 white Buick with its trunk open.

Are they from out of town? asked Fitzsimmons.

It's Marcus Hallston's boy. The nigger is some of Aunt Marzie's people. I figured they'd be out-of-town instigators so I called the newspaper.

They called me, said Fitzsimmons. What's your name, boy? he asked Larry Lime.

Larry Lime Beacon of Time Reckoning Breathe on Me Nolan.

Oh, one of them. What's your regular name?

Larry Lime Nolan.

You kin to Young, Marzie, that crowd?

Yessuh.

So you're Marcus's boy, Fitzsimmons said to Dwayne.

Yessir.

What's your name?

Dwayne.

And ain't you ashamed, young lady? he said to Linda.

Linda looked at the ground.

You're one lucky nigger, Larry, said Fitzsimmons. After your pictures are taken, Dwayne, you drive that Buick and your girlfriend on out of here now. Your daddy will be talking to you once he sees your picture in the Sunday paper. We'll hold it till Sunday. Better circulation, all that. You boys ought to be ashamed of yourselves. We'll call Young, get him in here to pick you up, boy, he said to Larry Lime.

Driving Larry Lime home, Uncle Young asked him, What the hell did you think you was doing? That's the wrong man to make mad.

Why?

'Cause he owns the world. That's who your mama works for.

Does he know her?

No.

Late the next afternoon, Saturday, the Amazing Rumblers loaded up the hearse at the furniture shop for the Bobby Lee Reese TV show. "The Amazing Rumblers" was written in white electrician's tape on the side of the black Cadillac hearse.

28

THE ACT BEFORE the eleven o'clock commercial break was Palmer Johnson, who sang and played guitar, backed vocally by thirteen-year-old Hazel Fitch, who went on to be the famous banjo picker. They did a song called "Supper Time."

The studio audience of fifty, some who'd stood in line for over two hours, applauded. The stage was only a foot high, and some had to crane their necks to get a good view of Palmer and Hazel.

After the commercial break, Baby Mercy and Bobby Lee came onstage.

Well, Bobby Lee, said Baby Mercy, how's Aunt Dormalee?

In his living room, Larry Lime said to his mama and daddy, I bet they coming on right after this.

She's fine, Bobby Lee said to Baby Mercy. And I can say this. She's been using the same box of Kleenex for as long as I can remember. That's Aunt Dormalee for you. She saw Uncle Bob pull up a Kleenex and blow his nose on it and throw it away, and she said, "Shame on you, Bob—just think of all the space for extra nose blows on that Kleenex," and Aunt Leotie was in the room and she said, "Shame on you, Dormalee. Why use a Kleenex when you can cut a handkerchief out of old, clean, worn-out underwear?" And they stood there looking at each other. Which is when Uncle Talmadge mumbled, "Why buy underwear?"

There was some laughter. Bobby Lee realized it wasn't the best audience he'd ever had.

And right *now*, ladies and gentlemen, we've got our amateur act of the week in the wings. Are they ready to come on, Baby Mercy?

Oh, yes, sir.

This is it, said Larry Lime. His brother and sister were in bed. His mama and daddy sat on the couch.

Ladies and gentlemen, said Bobby Lee, a band from right here in Starke. The Amazing Ram—Rumblers, hometown boys, doing "Hey Good Lookin'," a Hank

Williams song. And believe it or not, they were planning to bring along a chicken, a dancing chicken, but
the chicken couldn't make it. Next time, maybe. Come
on out, boys. And take it away.

He was talking 'bout Redbird, said Larry Lime, not
looking away from the TV screen where the Amazing
Rumblers were doing their first song.

We should have ate that chicken, said Booker.

Hey, Good Lookin', what you got cooking?
How's about cooking something up with me...

Bobby Lee walked onstage as soon as the song was
over. Hang on. Don't move, boys, he said. We might
get you to do another one. Is that possible?

Oh, yes, sir, said Dwayne. We've got a gospel tune.

This was the time for Bobby Lee to eat dog food,
and he did, tossing a dog food nugget high in the air
from behind his back. He had to try three times before
he caught a kernel in his mouth. Dwayne noticed
Bobby Lee's makeup, which made him look kind of
pasty in the bright lights.

And now, said Bobby Lee, let's hear another Hank
Williams tune, "I Saw the Light." A lot of people, said
Bobby Lee, don't know that Hank Williams wrote that
one too. Isn't that right, Dwayne?

Yes, sir. I guess. Well, I knew he sang it, but I didn't know he wrote it.

He sure did. Now, ladies and gentlemen, here they are, the Amazing Rumblers from Starke and Whittier, our very own, doing their rendition of "I Saw the Light." Take it away, boys.

Key of G. Dwayne counts it off. Mickey Dean is halfway through the lead-in. Dwayne seems to see something far away. He turns his back to the camera, faces the band, holds up his hand, and the band stumbles into silence. He whispers loudly, the "*Night* Train," turns and faces the camera, closes his eyes, and just like on the album he cries out, falsetto, *I say I lost someone.*

BA-BAM go the drums and cymbals.

Larry Lime jumps up off the couch. He's bathed in blue-gray light from the TV.

What the hell? says Booker.

Dwayne sings, *But I know where I'm gonna find them.*

BA-BAM. The whole band hits the full chords. They're with him — they are on autopilot.

All Aboard. Silence.

All Aboard. Silence.

All Aboard. Silence, and then...

All Hell Collapses on Live Camera and across TV

Land when Dwayne shouts, The *"Night* Train!" and drops his elbow as if into the midsection of someone attacking him, and the band commences that *BOOM BOOM DAH-DAH-DAH BOOM BOOM*—snare drum bapping loudly on the one and the two and a half.

Larry Lime is standing, leaning into the *one,* lifting and dropping his foot as if he's on the bass pedal, moving his head on the one. He says in a high voice, He *got* it, man. He *got* it. Did you hear that slip up to A-flat? Man.

Booker says, What the hell?

Larry Lime looks at his daddy. They doin' the "Night Train." They doin' the *"Night* Train."

Dwayne has his head down, his feet moving fast, and the whole place, the whole studio, the whole building has been turned exactly ... upside down, the studio audience stunned into silence as if shot dead. Some of the black audience out in TV land is also stunned— but stunned into shoulder movement, head movement. White boy gettin' *down.* He gettin' *down.*

And, oh, *oh,* Dwayne crosses one leg behind the other and does that 360-degree spin.

Larry Lime pretends to play along on drums, bamming his foot on that one beat. Booker looks from the TV to Larry Lime and back. What the hell? he says.

The sax and trumpet are blaring the "Night Train" riff. So dead on. And Dwayne is humped over with his eyes closed screaming in that screechy, coarse James Brown voice, and I mean this is some kind of smoking. Now he starts calling out the names of those cities: Miami, Florida; Atlanta, Georgia; Raleigh, North Carolina; and the band—*right now, as tight as a wasp's nest*—is doing that *whole band* beat on the one and on the two and a half every other measure, with the horns doing it too, and the syncopated pick-up beats on the off-measure. The band is a rocket ship sitting there a few yards off the launchpad, perpetually blasting, blasting, blasting off.

And up north of Starke, south of Whittier, at his mansion on the hill, Jared Fitzsimmons stands, puts out his cigar—a circular squashing in his big, green ashtray—puts on his nearest coat, and heads for the TV station.

Bobby Lee is standing just backstage, moving, kind of dancing. He smiles at Baby Mercy. Baby Mercy tries to smile, but it's hard because she has a sinking feeling about what is happening, and is about to happen.

BOBBY LEE REESE: *I was happy for it. I was happy it was happening. I don't suppose there were many white people in Starke over twenty-five years old who'd ever* heard of James Brown, much less that album. But I mean the Rumblers were tight, and that Dwayne Hall- ston was dancing like you ain't ever seen nobody but James Brown dance. Or I hadn't — at the time. He had to have been practicing those moves. Big time. I've never experienced anything like that since. Never will.

Of course it struck me at the end of the song, when maybe six people in the studio audience clapped their hands, that we'd delivered a dud of the century to that studio audience. I mean, I walked out onstage and I could practically hear what was being thought out there. I could feel the cement in the air. I mean, hell, chances are very high, regardless of the undoing — the changing — of, you know, racial-epitheted names of pet dogs and mountains and streams and sections of towns throughout the South since those days in the early sixties — chances are you'd be listening to what, as a white viewer in Starke, you called...not race music, but something worse. Something right there on your wet lips, all snappy, sassy, and peppy.

On camera, I sort of gained my composure. It was like, oh, I don't know, being at the best birthday party of your life and then the electricity goes out when you blow out the candles. Something like that.

What a fine performance, I said, you know, walk- ing out, sort of facing Dwayne, who was still James

Brown. He was still flushed, still moving back and forth on his feet kind of like a boxer getting instructions from the referee, a boxer who's a little worried about that other boxer facing him.

So I said to him, That song was by James Brown, wasn't it? Hell, I didn't know what else to say.

Yes, sir, he says. The hardest-working man in show business.

And by this time Baby Mercy is right there beside me. She sensed more than I did, I found out later. She grabbed my sleeve at the wrist and tugged and said, It's time to eat some dog food, Bobby Lee.

And then, still, it hadn't struck me that I was out of a job until Fitzsimmons got there after the show and told me I was fired. I can still see his face. And I said fine. I mean, something about that studio-audience reaction had already kind of pissed me off. Anyway, I'd never seen Fitzsimmons so flustered. It was like seeing a new, worse person.

Of course next day that newspaper photo came out showing Dwayne and that Nolan kid sitting at the drive-in in the front seat of a car on either side of a white girl. And then Monday morning the paper covered our "race show," and well, the rest is history. You got most of that written down from newspaper reports and all, don't you?

RAY WHEELER: *I do. And I still got my old band set lists.*

BOBBY LEE REESE: *I'm just glad the band got to keep on playing and you guys kind of made a name for yourselves with the album and with the* American Bandstand *gig.*

RAY WHEELER: *Oh, yeah, some of the best days of my life. I think about it a lot, but I need to ask you about photos. Do you have any? You know, of the show — acts, you eating dog food?*

BOBBY LEE REESE: *Four cigar boxes full.*

29

DURING THE WEEK following the photo in the Sunday *Prestonville Courier-News*, the Klan did a song and dance that scared some people. But there were no physical injuries.

Canary, on the Monday morning of the next week, walked along the path from her house. She walked by the church. Aunt Marzie had had a dream a few days earlier and told Canary all about it. The people who had gone to church at Liberty Day of Reckoning A.M.E. and had died were all buried in the graveyard behind the church and were going to rise up from the dead and come to the next grave cleaning, and Canary and Larry Lime were going to have to sing an Isaac Watts hymn and then "Down by the Riverside," and so they needed to practice. They practiced the songs, Aunt Marzie told Canary, but couldn't quite get all the words right, and Aunt Marzie decided to sing along with them. She woke up before they sang.

Canary walked across the tracks, by the back of the furniture shop and on by the Bone Brick Store, across the road, and to the front door of Flash's Mama's house. She knocked on the screen door. The inside door was open. She could hear Flash talking inside. When he opened the door, she saw that his hands were wet.

I'm washing her hair, he whispered. He seemed nervous or something.

Then he spoke up some. I just remembered last night, he said, that she hadn't had her hair washed in a long time. She always washed it at the sink.

I could have done that, said Canary. On the way to the kitchen, she was wondering how he was managing it—washing her hair with her in her half-paralyzed condition. In the kitchen, she saw. He'd lifted his mother up onto the counter. She was on her back, with her neck on a board over the sink so that the top of her head was next to the faucet.

Her eyes were half open, but only the whites showed. Her mouth was wide, wide open, and her face had no color.

Oh, my God, said Canary. She felt her knees weaken. She's dead, she said.

Flash said, It took her all night to die. She died about a hour ago, and I just got her up here like this. She don't weigh all that much no more. Flash braced himself with his hand against the sink and leaned forward and started dropping down, crying. Her toes is all curled up, he said. Look. He cried a full cry, then said, She wouldn't die and wouldn't die, and I kept saying the Lord's Prayer over and over. I said a line every time she breathed, and then there was a last breath, I thought, then another last breath, then one more, and then she was just gone. No more breathing, and I kept saying the Lord's Prayer over and over.

As Canary would tell it later:

Then he kind of half stood up from the floor where he was kneeling—he'd crumpled all the way to his knees, see—and I grabbed his stretched-out arm, and he said, Oh, God, can I hug you? and I said, Yes, of course.

On a Friday night a few weeks later, Larry Lime Nolan took his seat at the yellow Fender Rhodes electric piano. There was a crowd in the Frog. He placed his right thumb on the B-flat below middle C, his middle finger on the D just above, and his left little finger on the B-flat down below. He looked to the Bleeder, who nodded for Larry Lime to go ahead and count it off, to commence his own arrangement of "Blue Monk" with the Jazz Group behind him. The audience of fifty or so, some standing, was quiet. That's the way it was at the Frog.

Larry Lime was confident. His chest, head, and heart felt high above him. He was ready to feel the music's effect on other people. He had on a narrow-brimmed hat. He knew he was a jazz musician — and would be for the rest of his life.

Acknowledgments

Thanks to:

My editor, Pat Strachan; my agents, Liz Darhansoff and Lynn Pleshette; copyeditor Ben Allen; and to all the helpful folks at Little, Brown.

Friends and family for information, suggestions, insights, support: Vic Miller, Louis Rubin, James Johnson, Hilbert Campbell, Kristina Edgerton, Catherine Edgerton, David McGirt, Tom Rankin, George Terll, Buster Quin, Eric Porterfield, Sharon Boyd, Bill Blair, Joe Mann.

My students and fellow faculty members at UNCW.

Philip Gerard, David Cordle, and Rosemary DePaulo at UNCW.

Ed Paolantonio and his book on piano improvisation.

Adonna Thompson at the Duke University Medical Center Archives.

The Center for Documentary Studies at Duke University, Durham, North Carolina, especially for their work on the following two projects: *Behind the Veil: Documenting African American Life in the Jim Crow South* and *The Jazz Loft Project.*

Dr. Robin D. G. Kelley for his book on Thelonious Monk.

William Price Fox, Jim Thornton, O. C. Mitchell Jr., Crafton Mitchell, Mark Teachey, and Keith McLellan.

Friends who helped with retyping and other support: Lisa Bertini, Megan Hubbard, Melissa Rabon, Carmen Rodriguez, Janie Miller.

Jack King, Matt Kendrick, and Mike Craver of the Rank Strangers Band for their inspiration and love of music.

Those who supported the Fragile X Foundation and other charities through name auctions.

*   *   *

And for memories of gold, I'm forever grateful to:

The boys from the Seven Keys band:
    Dennis Hobby, lead singer
    Billy Russell, drums
    Darrell Schrum, trumpet
    Gerald Schrum, sax

John Nichols, guitar, vocals
Tommy Crabtree, electric bass

The boys from the Sierras band:
Melvin Dickerson, lead singer
Morris Stancil, guitar, vocals
Donnie Bissett, drums
Jimmy Wilson, electric bass, vocals

About the Author

CLYDE EDGERTON was born in Durham, North Carolina. He is the author of nine previous novels, including *Walking Across Egypt, Lunch at the Piccadilly,* and *The Bible Salesman.* He has been a Guggenheim Fellow and is a member of the Fellowship of Southern Writers. Edgerton teaches creative writing at the University of North Carolina Wilmington. He lives in Wilmington with his wife, Kristina, and their children.